Visiting Nurse

NURSE IN WHITE

LUCY AGNES HANCOCK

WILDSIDE PRESS

Nurse in White

Published by Wildside Press LLC
www.wildsidepress.com

TO NURSES EVERYWHERE

AND TO ALL

WHO MINISTER TO THE SICK IN BODY

AND IN MIND

Grace be yours and strength,
Patience and understanding,
Wisdom also and the priceless gift of laughter.
"Freely ye have received, freely give."

CHAPTER ONE

ELLEN GAYLORD, tenderly massaging her aching feet, frowned inhospitably as a fellow probationer hobbled into the room they temporarily shared. There were purple smudges beneath Ellen's brown eyes and her face looked white and tired. Solitude was what she longed for. Privacy in which to weep, wail, wallow in misery, free from sympathetic or amused glances.

"What a life—what a life!" Ann Murdock groaned loudly as she flung herself down on her cot. "If I had known—if I had but known!" She sat up abruptly at a sudden thought. "Say, Gaylord, if you'll anoint my feet, I'll anoint yours."

"Anoint? How do you mean, anoint?"

"Oil 'em, stupid. Oil's the best thing there is for tired feet. I ought to know—my dad's a mail carrier."

"No, thanks," Ellen murmured. All my feet need is rest and that's what they're going to get for the next ten hours. Ouch!"

Her eyes smarted with sudden, childish tears and she drew her feet up quickly. The rug was prickly, and as Ann was continually pointing out, probably crawling with germs; but of course that was nonsense in a hospital as scrupulously clean as Anthony Ware!

Now Ann laughed but quite without mirth. "Think you'll be able to stick it, babe?" she asked, curiously.

Ellen blinked rapidly. She knew she was a big baby; but just now she was terribly homesick. Michigan was a long way off. However, she had no intention of letting the other girl know how low she felt and her reply was short.

"Of course."

"No 'of course' about it." Ann spoke as one who knew a great deal about the subject. That was one of the many annoying things about Ann Murdock. "I bet you a new dime that a quarter of the class drop out when their three months are up, if Forsyth doesn't beat 'em to it and kick 'em out before. This hospital is noted for its tough training. I didn't know it when I entered; but—Jerusalem the Golden! how I know it now! Tell me, sweetheart, just why, for Pete's sake you ever decided to become a nurse, anyway? With your looks, plus that appealing artlessness, you ought to have been in the movies or married, ages ago. I bet you simply mowed them down."

"Why did you?" Ellen countered, ignoring the last.

"I asked first; but I don't mind telling you it was needs must in my case. You see, I happen to have two expensive half-brothers (nasty little brats!), a step-mother who thinks I'm a hussy, which fact I'm not disputing; no aptitude for anything in particular and am strong as a horse. I had the role of nurse in a play the Dramatic Guild put on last summer and I simply wowed them. The uniform was the cutest thing—only my innate modesty prevents my stating how vastly becoming it was to my exotic style. Suffice to say—I ran away with the entire show. Oh, that smart white frock and chic little cap! But ugh!" she wrinkled her nose in distaste as she stared down at her blue and white gingham, black cotton stockings and serviceable, low-heeled black oxfords. "Well, to skip the harrowing details, Step-mama sent to Anthony Ware for an application blank." Ann sighed gustily. Her voice became funeral. "Under pressure—here I am. Now, it's your turn, Gaylord. Tell all."

Ann lay sprawled on her narrow cot, her red hair spread fanwise over her flat pillow and her slender legs in their obnoxious covering, limp with fatigue. Ellen, still tenderly nursing her swollen, aching feet, eyed the other girl doubtfully. Better not tell her how all her life she had dreamed and hoped and planned on becoming a nurse. How, one by one, she had overcome the objections of her family who still held to the old belief that a girl had but one true mission in life—that of wife and mother. How at last with the aid of Aunt Bess, herself a trained nurse and the widow of Doctor John, Ellen's favorite relative, she had come east for training in Anthony Ware. Better not tell her of the feeling of exaltation she had experienced as she donned her ugly striped uniform for the first time and went down to breakfast with the rest of the staff. Better not tell her that a framed copy of the Florence Nightingale Pledge had hung in her room at home ever since she was ten; that it had been a part of her prayers each night, and now reposed, well hidden, in her trunk.

8

No, Ann Murdock wouldn't understand what being privileged to wear the badge of service, to belong to that glorious, heroic army known as "Trained Nurses," meant to her. Wouldn't understand that Ellen felt her call to the Work (with a capital W) as direct and as sacred as did any old time preacher of the Gospel. So she said slowly and simply:

"You see, I always wanted to be a doctor, but if not, a nurse anyway. My family tried to discourage me; but—well—here I am!"

"Thrilling!" mocked Ann and sent a shoe to one corner of the narrow room. "Wouldn't that make a swell movie, though? Proby realizes a life-long ambition! Gets blisters on her heels and fallen arches! I perceive, Gaylord, my pet, you're intensely emotional. Much too emotional, I'd say, to make a really good nurse; but I'll bet my best nighty you'll never acknowledge you're licked. Though they slay you, yet will you be true to your pledge. It's sure a shame to spoil a swell kid like you, Gay. You know, you've got to be hard-boiled as a longshoreman to stand a nurse's life. Three years from now—if we're still alive and on speaking terms, I'll be interested to comment on the transformation, or do we call it metabolism—being now among the elect?" Her other shoe followed its mate and she wriggled her toes experimentally.

Ellen watched the girl opposite with mixed feelings. She doubted if Ann was as hard as she tried to appear; but just the same, she was a little sorry that they had been assigned to the same room even for a short time. Ann ridiculed everything. Nothing was sacred and she professed to have little if any respect for anyone, be they doctors, supervisors, nurses or patients. She was quick and clever and did her full share of the hard and disagreeable tasks, but she did everything with the air of one making a concession to temporary powers-that-be, not as Ellen felt it should be done—happily, even devoutly, as one privileged to perform a beautiful and sacred duty.

"I doubt if I shall change much," she said confidently. "Uncle John was a doctor. He took his profession seriously and was one of the kindest, gentlest, tenderest men I ever knew."

"Was? Then he's dead? They always die," Ann stated positively. "It doesn't pay, my child. Sick people are vampires—they'll sap your strength—suck your life-blood if you let them. I bet your model uncle died young. Didn't he? How old was he?"

"Thirty-seven," Ellen answered and at Ann's triumphant: "There! What did I tell you?" went on: "He had a streptococcus."

But Ann wasn't convinced. "And was too gentle—too tender to throw it out of a system already weakened, no doubt, from giving of his strength and vitality to a whole flock of other parasites—human ones. I tell—"

"Nonsense!" Ellen interrupted sharply. "It just so happened that he was attending a re-union of his fraternity when he was stricken. The strep germ works fast—he hadn't a chance." She eyed her room-mate for a moment then said derisively: "I hope if I happen to get sick while I'm here, they won't assign you to the job of nursing me. I'm afraid you'd spoil me with too much coddling."

Ann laughed. "Don't get me wrong, darling. I'm really a swell nurse—theoretically."

"You're a swell fake, Ann Murdock!" Ann grinned at the other girl—suddenly understanding. "I suspect you enjoy listening to your own particular brand of hard-boiled philosophy, or whatever you call it. I bet you're positively maudlin on occasion—given the time, the place and the—er—"

"Ye-ah?" jeered Ann, peeling off the offending stockings and tossing them after her shoes — "especially when Angus rolls his r's and his eyes—don't you love his eyes, Gaylord?"

"Love them?" laughed Ellen. "Why, I've never even seen them. He scares the breath out of me when he even glances in my direction. I—I think he's positively awful—I mean awe-inspiring!"

"Pooh!" Ann scoofed. "Angus is just a man like other men, only perhaps a trifle more so. I never yet saw the man I'd stand in awe of. And by the way, would you be interested in a scrap of personal gossip, Angel? Believe it or not, my dear, I had a date with Bill Burgess last night."

"Burgess? You mean Doctor Burgess?"

"Absolutely. With the noble interne!"

"But Ann—it's against the rules—"

Ann laughed gleefully and kicked up her heels. "Haven't you ever heard that rules were made just to be broken, darling? But as it happened, the party wasn't worth the risk in this instance. We went over to Corinth. A bunch of medical students crashed the party and apparently a good time was had by all but Burgess. One or two of the medicos weren't half bad. There was one in particular they called Cy—tall and blond and terribly good looking and was he bored with the dumb bunny with him! I danced with him just once—he's a swell dancer—and then the noble Burgess pops up and says he's got to back—it's getting late. Blondie kidded him about being scared of Mac and Burgess had the nerve to blame it on me—said it was on my account. Imagine! As if I cared a hoot. As well be hung for a sheep as a lamb. The deed was done, why worry? But Burgess had to drag me away. What a pansy the great Burgess turned out to be! Take a tip from one who knows, Babe, pass up the internes—they're total losses, every time."

"I don't happen to be interested in men," Ellen rejoined, shortly.

"No-o? Then what kick do you expect to get out of this slavery, infant? Oh, pardon me, my error!" at the look of distaste in Ellen's face. "You're pledged to a life of toil and self-sacrifice. Pledged to emulate the noble life of our patron saint. We-ll." she yawned widely, turned on her stomach and reached under her cot for mules, "more power to you, Gaylord—if—ugh!—it's true, which I reserve the right as an American citizen, free, white and twenty-two— to doubt." She strolled over to the door then turned a face of mock tragedy. "If I do not return in one hour, please call Angus. I shall have gone to sleep in my bath and drowned, and I'm sure no one else could bring me back—that is, to a continuation of life in this bastile— but the strong, silent, masterful old Scotty—Lord love him! Don't mourn my passing too deeply, sweetheart—it is for the best, and please omit flowers. S'long!"

Ellen was laughing weakly when the door finally clicked

shut. Ann was funny. She yawned and stretched her arms above her head. Anthony Ware wasn't quite as bad as that. Surprisingly, her feet felt better and her nostalgia less poignant. She must write an amusing and interesting letter to her mother tonight. Must make her see only the beauty and happiness, if any, here at the hospital. Her mother must never guess that at autopsies her girl's legs still felt like boiled macaroni, that her throat often filled with tears at all the pain and suffering. She must be kept from suspecting that for more nights than she dared count, her youngest had cried herself to sleep from aching back, burning feet and missing them all at home.

Instead, she would tell her of this morning's chapel. Miss Forsyth, the soul of punctuality, was a little late but entered unhurriedly, followed by Doctor MacGowan and Doctor Braddock, the House Physician. She would try to give her the picture of the great stained glass window in the east wall. Christ healing the sick. "Freely ye have received—freely give." Make her feel the stillness that hung like a benediction over the shabby room.

" ' I will lift up mine eyes unto the hills, from whence cometh my help.' "

The slow, precise voice of Miss Forsyth led in the reading of the one hundred twenty-first psalm. Clear and strong came the voices of the staff in response:

" ' My help cometh from the Lord, which made heaven and earth.' "

" ' He that keepeth thee will not slumber.' "

These short chapel services after breakfast each morning were such a help—such perfect preparation for the day's work or for sleep after a night of labor. This morning she had glanced shyly about the rather bare room—her heart swelling with devotion. This was one of the pictures that would remain indelibly stamped on her memory. The erect, rather handsome, rather austere Superintendent in fresh, spotless white, flanked on either side by Chief Surgeon and House Physician, facing the staff—rows of uniformed nurses, internes, orderlies, dietitian, cook and maids—a goodly company.

How glad she was that despite bitter opposition, this old custom had been retained at Anthony Ware! She had heard that many of the modern hospitals had long since discarded morning chapel as old-fashioned—obsolete. She had studied the faces of her associates, many of them, like herself, tired to the point of exhaustion, but relaxing visibly as the reading went on to the twenty-third psalm—

" 'The Lord is my Shepherd; I shall not want —' "

" 'Yea, though I walk through the valley of the shadow of death, I will fear no evil—' "

A nurse so often was called to stand by while someone went down into that valley — stand by, sometimes, to summon them back to loved ones loath to have them go. " 'I will fear no evil — ' " She had murmured those words in her heart as she stood beside the sick. Not aloud, for Anthony Ware was non-sectarian and all classes, all creeds and those without creeds were treated there, and treated with the same care and devotion.

It seemed to her that every heart lifted as the staff took up the response:

" 'For Thou art with me; They rod and Thy staff they comfort me —' "

They had filed from the room, each to his own appointed task and she had gone down the hall to the elevator that was to take her to Male Medical, rested and eager for the day's work. All the misery and sorrow that had weighed so heavily on her heart such a short time ago, had fled.

Her mother would be interested to know that Miss Forsyth had smiled at her and asked her how things were going, when they met in the corridor one morning. That Doctor Angus MacGowan was tall and lank and ugly, a woman-hater and a worker of miracles. That the two internes were smart-alecky, just as she had known they would be. That Ann Murdock was always amusing but inclined to be fresh and more than a little meddlesome, although she liked her a lot. That the nurses were all grand but that Marcella Harris, a graduate nurse who had been at Anthony Ware for years, had been particularly sweet to her.

Oh, there were heaps of interesting and pleasant things to write home about.

CHAPTER TWO

ANN MURDOCK had been right in her prediction, for fully one-third of the September class of probationers failed to meet the Hospital's strict requirements and departed forthwith. Ellen stayed on and Ann Murdock — both high in their class.

The gingham uniforms and black shoes and stockings, *bete noire* of all probationers, were thankfully discarded in favor of white. On that first day, Ann did a gay little fandango before Ellen's mirror and cocked a roguish, mocking eye at Ellen whose glowing face proclaimed to all the world: "Now I am truly a nurse—a student to be sure, but still a nurse!"

As a queen wears her crown, sign of royalty, so Ellen donned the bit of snowy organdy—symbol of, to her, a far nobler calling, and though Ann jeered at Ellen's pride in her pert little cap, Ellen saw that she held her red head a little higher because of it.

The two no longer roomed together but across the hall from each other and Ann continued on her arrogant, self-willed way, making few friends among her associates because of her high-handed, hard-boiled manner, yet standing well in her classes and with the faculty in general.

Each new interne became her immediate prey, for a brief space, to be promptly dropped after a stolen date or two. The girls in the house soon creased to remonstrate and to warn. Ann apparently possessed a charmed life. She was never found out and, oddly enough, the men whom she disparagingly dubbed "pansies" were far more loyal to her than she was to them.

No one could understand Ellen's friendship for her. The two were so dissimilar. And yet as the months passed there was formed a strong and very real bond of deep affection between them. Sometimes to be sure, Ann's attitude of guardian—of self-appointed mentor, irked; but for the most part, Ellen submitted to the older girl's rather dictatorial manner with amused tolerance. Ann meant well. Ann was city born and bred and had all the urbanite's mistaken ideas of a country girl's inability to take care of herself. And it was Ann who stood close to Ellen during

14

that first day in the operating room when, as the gleaming knife in the hands of the Senior Surgeon's magic fingers cut cleanly through the pink flesh of a small boy, Ellen saw Doctor MacGowan rise and fall in the most fantastic manner and felt wave after wave of deathly nausea assail her. It was Ann who pinched her arm and kept her upright throughout the ordeal.

It was Ann who broke rules to come to her on that first Christmas Eve when small Eloise Baker slipped out of her scarred and tortured body and Thompson, the nurse in charge, became hysterical and fled. Thompson had grown to love that tiny, pain-racked baby and couldn't watch her die. It was Ellen's first experience with death and somehow, Ann, up in Male Surgical, had heard of the Thompson debacle and thought of Ellen—alone. She found her quietly bathing the little body while tears streamed down her face.

"You poor kid!" Ann whispered huskily.

"I—I'm not crying because I was left here alone, Ann," Ellen told her, "or because I'm afraid. I'm crying because I'm glad—glad that now Eloise won't have to suffer any more. Think of it, Ann—It's Christmas Eve and she's— she's got a brand new body!"

"You poor kid!" Ann repeated and stayed to help until Thompson, a white, shaken and vastly ashamed Thompson, returned.

Ellen couldn't forget that side of Ann's nature and chose to ignore the other side.

So the months passed. Months of hard work and rigid discipline. Months when nothing but Ellen's loyalty to her pledge kept her from open rebellion. For, being willing and more than ordinarily docile, some of the nurses took advantage and sometimes shifted their responsibility to her slender and already burdened shoulders. Ann called her an easy mark and all kinds of a sap, but Ellen refused to complain. So Ann deepened the enmity of several of her associates because she told them quite frankly what she thought of them and threatened to take it up with Forsyth or even MacGowan.

And as Ann lost favor with the girls in Anthony Ware, Ellen gained it. She was so willing—so smilingly happy in her work, that it was impossible to be with her and not feel one's spirits lift and one's outlook on life brighten. She was perhaps the most popular girl in training, and the prettiest.

Ellen's first year was suddenly completed; her second and part of her senior year. She had changed—grown up. She was still somewhat emotional—still felt keenly the dignity of her calling, but she had developed a firmness, only hinted at before, and a rather quick temper that surprised herself and delighted Ann.

Another September and a new crop of probationers — a new crop of internes. MacGowan's reputation took a sudden spurt after that famous operation on Senator McGill who had fallen from his horse and was thought to be fatally injured. "Miracle Man" he was called, much to his displeasure. Mac claimed no miraculous power. If he was vouchsafed more than average success in his operations, it was due to his steady nerves, clear brain and perfect co-ordination — together with the help of God. As a Scot and a strict Presbyterian, he was sure of Divine aid in his work simply because he never began an operation without beseeching that aid. Ann called him a simple soul with a one-track mind—surgery; but while the chief-of-staff was a successful surgeon, the knife was always to him the last resort — to be used only when other means failed. If he considered an operation necessary — an operation was performed; but if in his opinion, surgery was either useless or unnecessary, no power on earth could make him operate. There were doctors who called him pig-headed; specialists who sneered at what they dubbed his "know-it-all" attitude, urging the advancement of science as paramount to the loss of, a few years from a life, of even that life itself; patients who begged him to take a chance, willing to trust to his magic fingers; but he would not be swerved from his course.

Anthony Ware was proud of him. Other and larger hospitals made him flattering offers, all of which were declined with little or no thanks. When his seven years should be up, he was going back to Edinburgh to remain, two, five, perhaps ten years. He had learned much in America and would take that knowledge back to Scotland.

October — a crisp, frosty October morning with the sun turning the shabby little chapel into a glowing, colorful jewel. Ellen, who was on night duty, felt the quietness and beauty flow over her like a soothing bath. All too soon it was over and she walked along the lower hall to the side entrance on her way to the Nurses' Home. Ann Murdock fell into step.

"What did you think of the pair of them, Ellen?" she asked. "Not bad, eh what? Tall, blond and mischievous looks somehow familiar. I've been puzzling where I've seen him. He looks interesting anyway — not the usual pansy type Anthony Ware has been drawing. The redhead isn't so impossible, either. I quite enjoyed chapel this morning — usually it's just one long-drawn-out yarn. Guess I'll have to give them the once over, Angel. Want to date 'em with me? Next week we go on days for a change. Seems to me we get more than our share of night work. You may like it, but it cramps my style. What fun can one have in an afternoon?

When twilight draws her mystic curtain,
Revelry begins for certain.

Tip used to say it and it's true, I've found. My dear step-mama changed one word in it. She insisted it was deviltry that began with night-fall. Well, sometimes the two words are synonymous, but what of it? Will you come, Angel?"

Ellen felt suddenly deflated. Was that all Ann got out of chapel service? She felt Ann's eyes on her and refrained from showing her feelings. Anyway, she ought to know Ann — know her proneness to exaggerate and to depict herself in the character of *blase* woman of the world.

"Absolutely not, my child," she answered loftily. "I've all the troubles I can handle right now without adding to them. Go play with your little friends yourself, darling, but count me out."

Ann laughed. "I know," she jeered. "You're afraid of being found out. Oh, come on, Stiff-in-the-morals, I'll see you through."

17

"Some other time, Ann," Ellen put her off. "I think it would have to be something more thrilling than a new interne to make me risk losing my cap. Were they in chapel? I didn't notice."

"You wouldn't!" Ann exclaimed in disgust. "Why do you still stick to that 'holy orders' attitude, Ellen? Our job has to deal with bodies — very human, very earthly bodies, not with people's souls, if any. I can't for the life of me get any deep religious fervor from rubbing Old Phlebitis up in Male Medic or in listening to the temperamental outpourings of Old Vitriol down in Hades."

Ellen smiled good-naturedly. "You're funny, Ann. You're gentle as a mother when you massage that same Old Phlebitis and dutifully attentive to Mrs. Vitriol, as you call her, down in the Women's Surgical. You can't fool me any more, Ann Murdock. It's only your shell that's hard. Inside you're as soft as— as putty. And I'm not sanctimonious, Ann. I may have been once but not any more, and in spite of anything you may say to the contrary, I still think nursing is the noblest profession in the world, except, perhaps, medicine or surgery, and I'm proud I belong."

Ann gave her a quick hug. "You're a grand kid, Ellen, and I'm just a black ewe, but I love you just the same. S'long, precious — see you at dinner — perhaps."

Overnight, it seemed, the personnel of Anthony Ware had changed. Cyrus Dent, fresh from a year in Bellevue, tall, athletic, blond as a young god, swaggered (the term was Ellen's who suddenly and for no reason she could explain heartily disliked him) through the corridors, turning the heads of the susceptible younger nurses and raising the temperatures of many a female patient. Just as if Fielding, funny, redheaded Bob Fielding, wasn't menace enough for one season!

Ann quickly let it be known that the policy of "hands off" still prevailed. Bob immediately fell under her spell and ever after remained fraternally loyal to his fellow redhead. Cy wasn't interested for a time and Ann, who refused to acknowledge defeat where any man was concerned, persisted in her subtle wooing. Wasn't he an old acquaintance? She remembered him now — back when they were both still half-baked. Bets were laid with the odds on Ann. It wasn't long until the house knew that she was meeting Cy two blocks around the corner, where his car was parked.

Doctor Dent's attitude toward Ellen was one of amused condescension and that young lady found herself trembling with rage at the gleam of mirth in his eyes as he paused to watch her gently bathing the face of some crusty old codger or attempting to soothe an irritable harriban. She tried ignoring his presence but he would somehow manage to get in her way. She became coolly polite and formal only to have to have him laugh mockingly. She even took a leaf from his own and Ann's book — tried being flippant and answered his jibes in kind.

"You're out of character, Nightingale," he would chide. "You are much better in the title role."

And Ellen, fighting tears of rage and humiliation that she had let him know that he could upset her, would flee before his amused chuckles. Then it was that Ellen wished she were more like other girls—less devoted to a Cause—less old-fashioned, naive and sincere. She would beat her hands together in impotent rage. If only she could hurt him in some way! If only she had some weapon that would wipe that hateful smirk from his classic mouth and bow that blond head low! She felt powerless to combat him and despised herself for her lack of self-control, she who had been so aloof—so impervious to everything male.

Suddenly, he began appearing around midnight when she was on night duty, with uncanny skill choosing a time when she was alone or managing to find an errand for the girl on duty with her so that the meeting had all the appearance of a rendezvous. She could not make a complaint—it was all so trivial and childish. Perhaps he would grow tired of heckling her and turn to someone else. She had only to keep a stiff upper lip and refuse to let him know he annoyed her. The old formula she had used as a child failed her here. Then, she would say over and over again: "They can't hurt me — no one can hurt me—I refuse to be hurt." Now it had no potency. Cyrus Dent did hurt her—hurt her pride and her dignity.

She fancied the other girls eyed her with amusement and no little envy and she felt once or twice that even the House

Physician looked disapprovingly at her. But what could she do? Ann apparently saw nothing amiss, and went on her way as if young Dent were already her abject slave. Perhaps she only imagined it all, Ellen would tell herself miserably. Perhaps she was exaggerating his attention. In that case, the cure should be certain. She had only to refuse to notice him at all.

She would feel better after that decision and for a time it would seem to work. She would grin to herself as she saw the young man bite his lip and frown in perplexity when she failed to hear him when he spoke to her. She'd show him! Handsome men had always irked her and she yearned to put Doctor Cyrus Dent in his place—definitely and finally. Let him keep on haunting her locality if he wished and much good would it do him!

CHAPTER THREE

THE CLOCK ON the bank building had just struck twelve strident notes. Midnight, and Anthony Ware Hospital, sprawling on top of Main Street hill, blinked sleepily. Three hours before it had been wide awake, its five shabby stories ablaze with light, dominating the town that dozed at its feet. In the Receiving Room opening off the concrete court in the rear, light streamed from the long uncurtained windows. Inside, slim young nurse Gaylord and plump, not so young Doctor Braddock worked over a disreputable man who claimed to have been the victim of a hit-and-run driver. The name and address he gave were unquestionably fictitious. Not for a moment did either member of the staff believe him, but they had grown used to such things and his record was completed as if he were indeed the John Smith he claimed to be. Just another heel getting free treatment. That was the worst of an endowed hospital. Every chiseler in the vicinity felt it his right to get all he could for as little as possible.

However, John Smith's injuries were carefully treated and he shrugged into his coat muttering his surly thanks into a week's growth of beard. He had nearly reached the door before he asked grudgingly:

"How much, Doc?" He turned and his uninjured hand went into the torn pocket of his shabby trousers. He nodded to Ellen. "A neat job, Miss. Well, how much?"

"Why—why—" stammered Braddock surprised. "Can —do you want to pay? You know—"

"Sure I want to pay," John Smith growled with wholly unexpected and indignant pride. "I ain't no charity case. I pays fer what I gets, see? How much?"

"Mm—mm shall we say three dollars? That's about what your family doctor would charge."

"Okay." John Smith peeled three soiled bills from a small roll and handed them to the doctor. "Thanks," he muttered again surlily, and shuffled out into the night.

"Well!" Doctor Braddock grinned. "One never can tell an honest man from his exterior, can one?" His blue eyes twinkled. "Let that be a lesson to you, Gaylord."

Ellen, who had been cleaning up, suddenly stopped. She began searching along the floor and amid the paraphernalia on the long table. In the next room she could hear Mary Trent moving about replacing the instruments used in the last emergency case—a messy one. She was splashing a good deal of water and humming softly as she swished. Ellen went to the door and asked a question, then returned to continue her search.

"Lost something?" the doctor asked, busy scrubbing his hands.

"Only a clinical thermometer and a pair of expensive scissors. Three dollars—umph! He got them cheap." Her brown eyes met the startled blue ones of the fat little House Physician and the two went into a paroxysm of helpless laughter. "And let that be a lesson to you, Doctor Braddock," Ellen gasped.

"I thought there was something fishy about that guy—he had all the earmarks of a heel," the doctor said. "Well, I wasn't mistaken—that's something."

"Better make sure the three dollar bills aren't phony, too," Ellen reminded him, skeptically.

"I'll soon find out. I owe Mac five bucks—this three'll pay part of it. Trust a Scotsman to know if they're counterfeit or not. I wouldn't have Anthony Ware lose out, Gaylord—not for a moment."

Cyrus Dent wasn't coming tonight, thank goodness! Mary Trent was a long time cleaning up. Ellen wondered if he was deliberately keeping out of the way, but called herself a self-conscious idiot for dreaming such a thing. If the idea she wanted none of him had at last penetrated his thick skull, it was something. Ellen sighed with what she felt sure was relief.

"Poor Anthony Ware always loses, Doctor," she said, resolutely putting the young interne out of her mind. "It can't win. And how about the thermometer and scissors?"

"We-ll, there's always a certain amount charged to profit and loss each year. In a concern of this kind there's bound to be." The little man eyed the pretty nurse with concern. "You're not really worried about it are you, Gaylord?"

"Worried?" shrugged Ellen. "Why should I worry? It isn't my money; but it burns me up to be taken in—that I ever allowed such a stupid thing to happen. How could it have, Doctor? How could he have taken them with both of us right here?"

"What's up, Doc? You look concerned. Don't tell me that Gaylord's been saucy to you, too!"

Oh, that hateful chuckle! Ellen felt the blood rush to her cheeks and she shut her eyes tightly to hide the rage she knew burned in them. Oh, dear! Now she was in for another trying time and it upset her so!

Doctor Braddock frowned. Sometimes he felt this good-looking youngster was a bit brash. It wasn't seemingly in a young interne and he wondered if Mac had noticed it.

"Miss Gaylord is never saucy, Doctor Dent," he said with dignity and stalked from the room.

"Just like a bantam cock," grinned Dent, hooking a white-clad knee over a corner of the long table where he could watch the color ebb and flow beneath Ellen's clear skin. "Jove!" he said to himself, "the girl is lovely!"

"But he's such a peach!" Ellen defended loyally. "We're all crazy about him."

Cy slid along the table and laid his hand over hers. "Why waste your affection on old Braddock—a flat little benedict, Gaylord?" he whispered. "Don't—" he began softly then drew back hastily as the door opened.

"Hm—er—your lunch, Gaylord." Marcella Harris set down her tray with a thump and marched from the room —head high and eyes straight ahead.

"O—oh!" whispered Ellen in a stricken voice. "How could you!"

"O—oh!" the young interne mimicked and laughed. "Surely you don't mind a good, harmless little soul like Harris seeing me—er—well, sort of making friendly advances toward you, do you?" he chided. "Now if it were Agatha Forsyth, my child, or even mild Hattie Williams— now there's a gal! Knows her place—the cozy nook off Hades. Does she ever go the rounds? I hope not, but in either case it would be something else again, or if, perhaps, I should happen to be caught doing what I really want to do. But what possible objecttion can anyone have to our spending a minute or two in each other's company? I ask you. Don't be so strait-laced, Nightingale. We're only young once and—"

Ellen's heart hammered in her breast and she knew from Cy's twinkling eyes that he knew it. She drew away and clasped her hands tightly behind her back to still their trembling. How she hated this smiling, assured young doctor!

"I happen to be on duty, Doctor Dent," she managed, coldly, "and I certainly do not like—"

"So am I on duty but I do like," the young man laughed. "Be your age and generation, gal! Stolen fruit is always sweetest—I like it best."

"Well," said Ellen sturdily, "I don't. And I don't like feeling guilty."

Cyrus Dent chuckled again and Ellen bit her lip in annoyance at the slip.

"But why should you feel guilty, darling?" the young man drawled in that hateful mocking voice—and Ellen suddenly saw red.

"Because you have no business here, and"—she went on blindly—"disliking you as I do, I have no wish to have your presence misunderstood. Please go."

"Ah—ah—be careful, Nightingale," he teased, quite unoffended. Then insinuatingly. "Sure you don't like me— mm? Even a little bit, darling? Not even a little smitch?"

Ellen's brown eyes blazed into his blue ones for a moment and she choked—"I—I hate you!"

But Doctor Dent cried involuntarily: "Jove, you're lovely, Nightingale!"

A car shrieked to a stop just outside and Ellen, thankful for the interruption, flew to the door. Doctor Dent followed. Braddock, who appeared almost at once, betrayed no knowledge of the rendezvous and although he disliked Dent's methods and his exposing Ellen to a possible reprimand, he would never report what he knew of the affair. He liked Ellen Gaylord and didn't want to see her hurt, and if he knew anything about men, he feared that Cy Dent was a philanderer.

The man they brought in was badly battered, a leg broken in two places and a deep laceration over one eye. Ellen was surprised at the change in young Dent—at the speed and efficiency with which he worked—almost like Doctor MacGowan, she thought. But of course this was nothing— simple compared with things the surgeon did. The man was taken to the service elevator and shot up to a private room on the third floor. Ellen, Mary and the two doctors scrubbed themselves amicably and for once Cyrus Dent forebore

24

his teasing manner. Doctor Dent departed on his midnight round of specials and Doctor Braddock went into his own small laboratory off Emergency. Ellen and Mary Trent sat down to cold coffee and sandwiches. Mary ate with her eyes on her text book, Ellen drank cold coffee and let her mind wander.

"Did you hear that Dent has a swell job in Boston?" Mary asked suddenly and Ellen jumped.

"Has he?" Ellen was quite indifferent.

"With some ritzy specialist—nerves. I forgot his name."

"It doesn't matter," Ellen said. The other girl glanced at her, then down at her book.

Well, Ellen said to herself scornfully, this is the day of specialists. He'd be in his element hob-nobbing with a lot of silly women. Young Dent was soft—looking for an easy jb and easy money. Probably become a popular woman's doctor—listening to a recital of their ailments, real and imaginery, at a huge fee per recital. She could see him in her imagination—lolling at ease in his luxurious offices, while a stream of idle, perfumed, foolish, exotic women passed before him, each unconsciously taking with her as she left, a portion of his manhood, leaving him more and more the spoiled plaything of society. What a waste! Uncle John had been a country doctor and Uncle John was still Ellen's ideal of what a doctor should be.

Her thoughts swung to Doctor MacGowan and then to Miss Forsyth. Was the Superintendent really a man-hater? Did it follow that just because a person didn't marry he must necessarily dislike the other sex? She didn't think so. In fact, she had a strong suspicion that Miss Forsyth admired the plump little House Physician. It seemed as if her voice changed—softened and mellowed when she spoke to him.

Poor Doctor Braddock with his peevish, demanding, neurotic wife! Life was rather a mess at times. The wrong people tied together. What a grand wife Miss Forsyth would have made for the House Physician! To be sure she was taller and perhaps a year or two older, but what did that matter when they were both so splendid? Let the other girls poke fun at the Superintendent and Doctor Dent sneer at the House Physician, Ellen knew them for what they were, fine, strong and sincere; devoting their lives to helping the sick and, in addition, spending endless hours trying to imbue their students with something of the same helpful spirit. A sadly hopeless task in some cases, Ellen knew.

A telephone rang and almost simultaneously, the ambulance left the courtyard. Mary Trent tossed her text book aside and yawned sleepily. Ellen, whose thoughts were becoming somewhat muddled, jerked to attention. Braddock came in from the laboratory, one sleeve of his white coat scorched and stained. Ellen smiled at him.

"Hear where it went?" he asked her.

"No. It's been so unusually quiet tonight that we're probably in for a mob scene now O-oh, here it comes! Must have been close."

But the ambulance was empty. The woman was already dead when the ambulance had arrived and both driver and interne were sleepily truculent.

Five o'clock. Braddock went back to the lab and his own private experimenting. Doctor Fielding and the orderly drifted away. Mary picked up her text book and Ellen brought out a card index. It was a long two hours until seven. This had been an unusually tiresome trick—only six cases when twenty was merely a fair average. Ellen wondered where Cyrus Dent had gone. Probably up to seventy-nine where the Webster girl was recovering from a ruptured appendix. There were two specials on her case—both from Corinth. Well, what of it? Corinth General couldn't produce them any better than Anthony Ware, nor as good for that matter. But of course visiting girls are always more popular, Ellen knew, and she knew also that both specials were exceptionally pretty girls. Well, what did she care? Cyrus Dent was nothing to her.

"Hist!" Ellen turned sharply. Mary, after a sly look beneath her lashes, went on studying diligently—a frown of concentration on her brow. Ellen's face flamed. "Hist!" came again, somewhat more pronounced and Ellen went over to the door.

"Well?" she demanded coldly.

"I hope it is well. Say, come on over to Butternut Grove with me this afternoon. I'll take a lunch and we'll view the landscape and invite our souls."

"Thank you, Doctor Dent, but—"

"Are you human, woman? Is there a heart in your

26

boozum? Have you a soul? Give me ten good reasons why you won't come?"

"One will be sufficient. Rules," Ellen said icily. "I happen to feel like obeying the rules of the Hospital, that's all."

"Oh, thank heaven it's only that. I was afraid it was something personal. That maybe you didn't like me."

"I don't," Ellen said bluntly. "I think you are presumptuous and—and fresh!"

"Well, and what if I am? Surely you could never come to care for a chap who was stale, shall we say? Oh, come on, Nightingale, it's time to defrost. We could have a lot of fun. I'll meet you just around the corner and we'll be back by six-thirty. Come on, it's going to be a swell day— I personally saw to that—"

"You did?" Ellen jeered. "Listen!"

Icy particles struck the window and somewhere a shutter banged. Cy looked dashed for a moment but recovered almost at once.

"We could go to the Club and dance—"

"And have half the town dropping in—"

"What of it? I'll take the blame. I'll square it with the bosses—"

"That won't be necessary for I'm not going." Ellen spoke with quiet decision but inside she felt a wild yearning to accept.

The young interne turned her around and examined her face closely.

"Really, Gaylord, I can't understand you. You're a paradox. Young, beautiful, attractive and yet you have such low H and DQ's—'way, 'way down. Let's see, I'd rate you as sub-sub-normal. Too bad in one so very lovely. Unutterably sad—tragic."

"H and DQ's?" Ellen's brow wrinkled in perplexity.

"If you don't know what HQ stand for, Nightingale, your IQ is off, too." His laugh showed exasperation. "Do you know, Gaylord, I'm afraid that some day you'll tempt me beyond my powers of control and I'll do something about it."

Ellen's head went up and her brown eyes flashed dangerously.

"All I ask is that you let me absolutely and entirely alone, Doctor Dent."

"Oh, Nightingale! Not absolutely," his breath caught in a mock sob of distress. "Cruel—cruel wrench! You break my heart—feel the crack."

He caught her hand and pressed it against his chest. "Feel it?" he asked.

"No. I don't even feel your heart beat. Maybe you haven't one—maybe—"

"We-ll, as a matter of fact I haven't," he grinned at her. "I'll tell you a secret. It's just an aching void in there, darling, believe it or not. It was snitched and the place is now for rent. Know of a good tennant?"

"No, I don't," Ellen said shortly, "and I'm too busy to listen to your nonsense."

"Nonsense, she calls it! It's tragic!"

"Well, don't expect me to weep. Tell your troubles to the one who has your heart."

Cy grinned again. "Dear, sweet, Nightingale!" he whispered. "What a woman you are! Always so sympathetic, so kind and helpful! That's just what I shall do, and if sometimes I forget and haunt your presence, please understand that she—SHE has been especially cruel to me and I crave your sympathy and the healing magic of your sweet and friendly smile, so be a little forebearing."

A car slid to a stop in the drive with a squealing of brakes and Ellen slipped back into the Receiving Room. Mary Trent's eyes were quizzical. Doctor Dent bustled in as the occupant of the car entered. He was supposed to be making the rounds, darn him!

"Ripped the dressing from my leg, Doc," the man said as he came in.

"Okay. Let's have a look."

Doctor Braddock poked his head in at the door and ducked out again. Mary Trent went on with her studying and Ellen brought gauze, antiseptic solution and adhesive. Dent worked deftly and the man stood up after the job was done.

"Thanks, Doc," he muttered. "That feels better," and he started for the door.

"Cost you one dollar, brother," Cy said crisply.

"Aw, now Doc," the other whined. "I been outta work an'—well—I just ain't got a dollar."

"All right. We'll send you a bill and we'll expect you to pay. Understand?" Ellen was surprised at the firmness with which he spoke. "And you have got a job—that's why you're out so early. I'm keeping tabs on some of you guys who think this hospital runs for your especial benefit. That's seventeen dollars you owe, and you'd better be prepared to pay something this payday."

"Free hospital!" grunted the man, sidling toward the door. "Free nothin'. Rob yuh right an' left. A dollar fer a scrap o' rag an' a drop o' colored water! Free! Bah!" The door slammed after him as he went out into the gray morning.

"Chiseler!" grunted Cy Dent as he washed his hands. Ellen said nothing and after a long and exceedingly gushy sigh, he went out.

Mary Trent giggled and after a moment Ellen joined her. It was all so utterly silly! Why did she let him annoy her? Was he really in love with some girl? If it was true, why did he pester her so persistently? She examined the hand that had been held so tightly against Cy's heart—examined it curiously as if the answer lay in its pink palm.

"I believe you're spoofing, Doctor Cyrus Dent," she said to herself as she gave the offending hand an extra scrub, "and if you think for one minute I shall ever take you seriously, you're vastly mistaken. There is no place in my busy life for men—not for years and years—if ever. And I'm especially not interested in good-looking young doctors —blond ones in particular."

CHAPTER FOUR

"Cometh the zero hour and I'm slowly starving," Ellen wrote. "We had stew for dinner last night and you know how I loathe stews of all kinds, shapes and conditions. It's exactly ten minutes to one and if food doesn't arrive soon I shall do something desperate, like snitching a couple of chocolates from the little French girl who arrived yesterday. She shouldn't eat candy, anyway. I saw her hide the box under her pillow, just as if we didn't know! But perhaps she likes to feel it's there even if she isn't allowed to eat sweets. Poor youngster, (she can't be more than twenty). Valvular heart disease and diabetes melitus, as if one wasn't bad enough!

"Hold everything: I hear faint sounds. 'Tis the elevator coming up!"

Marcella Harris stepped from the electric elevator; reached inside for the tray; slid shut the door and hurried along the dimly lighted corridor to the alcove about half-way down, where Ellen sat at a table writing her weekly letter home. A pile of charts covering the sixteen patients in Ward L lay before her. Marcella's cap was slightly awry and there was a smudge (was it salad dressing?) on the front of her otherwise spotless uniform.

"You're a direct answer to prayer, Marcy," Ellen smiled. "What have we?"

Grilled ham sandwiches, cream cheese sandwiches made with brown bread—you like those; some of that good cake left from the auxiliary luncheon, and superfine coffee, warranted to float an egg. Okay? I snitched the cake and hid it. You gals on nights here in L rate a few luxuries, sez I. Where's Murdock?

"Receiving," Ellen explained, biting into a sandwich. "She said she'd be gone only a few minutes, but it's half an hour already. It's all right, though. Everything's quiet— for a wonder. Grand food, darling. What's new?"

Marcella perched on one corner of the table and swung a white shod foot.

"Not much. Dent's on ambulance duty—swapped with Fielding who hurt his ankle yesterday afternoon. So—I'm afraid Murdock's visit is quite useless. I wonder why someone doesn't put her wise."

Ellen smiled and sipped the fragrant coffee. Marcella didn't care for Ann. "Oh, it's all too—too childish, Marcy. The chances are Dent doesn't know Ann's alive any more." She knew that Ann and Cyrus had not been seeing much of each other lately. She herself had succeeded in avoiding him to some extent, and she wondered if he had noticed. One thing she was certain of, Ann's heart wasn't involved. It was just that a man—any man, was necessary to Ann's happiness. Just now, it happened to be Doctor Dent. And it was in all probability just as Doctor Braddock had pointed out to her, carefully and more or less diplomatically, that Doctor Dent had it in himself to go far. With his personality and looks, he would probably seek a wife who could aid him materially—one of the youngsters who chased after him at the Country Club for instance. Ellen felt instinctively that he was giving her a gentle hint not to allow Cy to turn her head. Well, she felt like telling him he needn't worry, though she said nothing. Of course those times when Cy had persisted in bothering her may have been misleading, but she didn't intend doing any explaining even to the House Physician.

"Sez you!" Marcella scoffed. "The man doesn't live who is immune to the flattery of a pretty girl's wide-eyed admiration, especially when that girl is redheaded and is provocative like Ann Murdock. I will say, though, that the glamorous Cy's interests still seem to be fairly well distributed elsewhere, and me thinks Mistress Ann is due for a bump."

"So?" Ellen asked and was annoyed at the guilty blush that made her suddenly uncomfortable. Perhaps Harris, too, had the crazy idea that Cy actually liked her instead of just —well—getting in her hair for the fun it provided him. Again she couldn't explain.

Marcella stared at the lovely face opposite and misunderstood the blush. Was it possible that Ellen didn't know that Dent was just a kidder? That he couldn't be serious if he tried? That he would without doubt look much higher in the social scale than that of a nurse when he was ready to take the fatal step? In fact, the story went that the debutante daughter of the town's wealthiest man was rushing him. They were often seen together at the Country Club.

The sandwiches were exceptionally good or else Ellen was more than ordinarily hungry, for the blush slowly receded and she appeared quite unmoved. Marcella kicked her heel against the table leg. She had to find out and if Ellen was actually soft on the big, good-looking bluff, she would put her wise even if it cost her their friendship.

"Oh, come now, Ellen. You can't pull the wool over my old eyes, you know. I know you're a bit on the reserved and 'aughty side, but I have intuition and all my faculties still. Aren't you and the handsome Cy—"

"I happen not to be interested in Doctor Dent, Marcella," Ellen said coolly. "But if I was, would it be a sin?"

"Not a sin, exactly; but I'd call it indiscreet or maybe even imprudent, like casting pearls before swine, if you know what I mean. Any girl's a sap—Oh-oh, here comes Murdock," as the elevator again slid to a stop and Ann Murdock hurried toward them. "How's the—er—palpitation?"

"Girls, Robert Cooper's down in Receiving!"

"The actor?"

"Who else? It seems he was in an accident—hurt his knee. Gee! Don't I have the darndest luck? The month I'm down there nights, nothing more romantic than a few battered small town drunks, the usual number of messy accident cases happen along and the saintly old rector of Saint John's with a first class shiner—you know the time. He ran into a door, or so he said. And here, the first week I'm back on ward duty, Robert Cooper drops in."

"Oh, woe is you!" Marcella mocked.

"Is he staying?" Ellen asked.

"No, worse luck! Old Braddock is fixing him up so he can go straight on to Chicago by plane. Girls, he's the best looking thing! Handsomer even than his pictures."

Marcella grinned slyly. "Better looking than Dent?"

"Oh, I wouldn't say that Cy Dent is the handsomest man in the world exactly," Ann retorted unperturbed, "but unquestionably he has that certain something—"

Ellen agreed that without doubt Cy did possess that certain something. She wished Ann would stop making an idiot of herself over him. He wasn't worth it. The faint whirring of the ascending elevator brought three pairs of eyes to the end of the dim corridor. Doctor Dent stepped

32

off and came toward them, a friendly grin on his handsome face.

"Speaking of devils—" Marcella muttered.

"Sister, can you spare a bite?" he whined ingratiatingly, his fine blue eyes on Ellen. But it was Ann who snatched up the plate of sandwiches and held them out to him. Marcella glowered. His own lunch was downstairs. But the young man, appearing not to understand her scowl, sent her a bland and somewhat mocking smile as he poured himself a cup of coffee in the cup intended for Ann who, strangely and to Ellen's astonishment, was far too excited either to eat or drink.

"Was it actually Robert Cooper, Doc?" Marcella inquired.

"Robert Cooper? Where?"

"In the Receiving Room just now. With a busted leg or something. Murdock here is all of a-dither."

Doctor Dent shifted his gaze to Ann, who promptly denied the allegation. "Do you mean the fellow Braddock routed Tony out for—the chap who had to be in Chicago by morning?"

"Yes—yes. Robert Cooper."

Dent grinned as he took a third sandwich. "If he was, he's traveling incognito. The name he gave Burns was Terrill Morley, 27, engineer, residence Boston."

Ellen and Marcella hooted softly. "Your imagination seems to be working overtime again, Murdock," Marcella jeered. "Probably looks as much like Cooper as I do Garbo."

"Well, he did," insisted Ann. "I guess I ought to know. I saw him, and I bet that's just it. He's incognito."

"Rather a good looking chap," Dent conceded magnanimously, "and he had a mighty bad knee. Braddock nearly wept when he insisted on going on—warned him against using it for a couple of months—you know what an old granny he is. But it was all wasted. The fellow looked mulish. 'That's all right, Doctor. Now bring on your chauffeur. I've got to get that plane', " Dent drawled with an exaggerated nasal down-east accent.

Ann indignantly protested he didn't talk like that at all. A light flashed red and Ellen left them. She was back almost at once, however, and poured herself a second cup of coffee.

"How's Lady X coming?" Dent asked, reaching for cake and remaining subbornly oblivious to Harris' open displeasure.

Ellen shook her head sadly. "She doesn't seem to be coming at all, Doctor. She's so terribly languid—so apathetic—doesn't seem to have the strength or desire to even try to live."

"I was afraid of that," he said. "She appeared licked from the start. No vitality—no endurance. But I did hope those transfusions—" He broke off, then "No clues, I suppose? Has MacGowan seen her lately?"

"Yesterday."

"Did he say anything?"

Ellen shook her head again. Marcella shrugged. It was Ann, an Ann roused and suddenly animated—intensely concerned over the unknown patient in whom Dent was obviously interested.

"Say anything! Does he ever say anything beyond the briefest of instructions? We're not supposed to have any interest in our patients as human beings—just as cases. The man's a machine—a robot. A clever one I'll admit, but still a machine. I've never seen a sign of human emotion in him in the more than two years I've been here. Have you?"

Doctor Dent put down his empty cup and brushed an imaginary crumb from the lapel of his spotless white coat. "We-ll, Murdock," he drawled, his manner judicial, "it depends on just what you call 'human emotion.' I've never seen him—er—kissing—say, Miss Forsyth, for example, or chucking you under the chin; but for all that he's a darned fine surgeon in his particular field and it wouldn't surprise me in the least if what the medical journals say of him is true—that he's just about tops in his special line. To lesser folk, Angus no doubt appears something of a god."

Ann looked distainful. "That's all right, Doc, but I'd think a lot more of him if he was less god and more man."

"No, doubt about that," grinned Marcella wickedly, and picked up the tray. Ann had eaten little or nothing, but that was her affair. If she was silly enough to get all hot and bothered over every male creature who came within a mile of her, Marcella determined that it should not interfere with her schedule. Ann was the limit and how she ever got into

Anthony Ware was a mystery to her. She stalked to the elevator shaft, pressed the button and watched the car ascend. She deposited the tray and waited to see if Dent was going downstairs where he belonged. Apparently he hadn't finished what he had come for. Well, she could wait. She wished he wasn't so darned good looking and she wished he had picked anyone but Ellen Gaylord. Ellen was much too sweet to be tricked as she was sure he was tricking her every day of his life. Marcella's plain little face darkened belligerently. "I'd like to wring his neck!" she muttered. "Why are the nicest girls the biggest saps?" She wished he had really fallen for Murdock. She was a match for him. Look at him now, darn him!

Ann had sputtered angrily at Marcella's gibe: "You know what I mean, Marcella Harris," and glared at the young interne as he grinned into her face. "And you know, too. MacGowan's an old crab and I don't care who knows I think so."

"S-sh-sh!" admonished Dent. "Not so loud, my girl. And I'm sure Gaylord here doesn't agree with you."

"No," said Ellen stoutly, "I don't. I think Doctor Mac-Gowan is wonderful and I adore working with him. Was there something in particular you wanted, Doctor?" she asked coolly as Dent lingered in spite of Marcella's attitude of exaggerated patience as she waited at the elevator.

"Er—no—oh, no. Just had a free moment and thought I might get a bite to eat up here." His laugh was exasperated. Why didn't those two leave and let him have a few minutes alone with Ellen? "I know Harris' penchant for Ward L —or rather the nurses at present on this ward. And I hate eating alone."

"Umph!" snorted Ann, still peeved. "You might have brought your own lunch along. You gypped me out of mine, I notice."

"Did I? Gee, that's tough, Murdock! Why did you stop me?"

"Stop you! How could I? I never saw food disappear so fast in my life."

"Want me to send mine up to you?" he asked as he motioned Marcella that he was going down. "Anyway, thanks for the handout," he called back.

"Hope he chokes!" muttered Ann as she watched him enter the elevator. "A typical interne—a typical man. Selfish brutes!"

Ellen picked up her fountain pen. "Aren't we all?" she asked. "And you should not have allowed him to eat your lunch, Ann. Breakfast is a long way off."

"You're telling me!" complained the other, then brightened. "Maybe Slavonski'll give me an orange if I hint long enough." She got up to answer as a red light glowed. "That's Slavonski now. Probably wants another orange—and here's where I eat."

Ellen finished her letter to her mother in Michigan, slipped it into an envelope, stamped and addressed it and watched it slide down the mail chute. No news this week. Except for the advent of the unknown young woman who lay in a plaster cast at one end of the long free ward—nothing especially interesting had occurred in the hospital for days. The same old grind. If only that strangely appealing patient could give them some clue to her identity! Another summons and Ellen slipped down the long room to the semi-privacy of the unknown patient's bed.

The great eyes were open with that same strange look in their purple depths — half terror — half inquiry.

"What is it dear?" Ellen asked, softly smoothing back the bright hair from the thin face on the flat pillow.

"Could — could you please stay with me — a little while? I am fr — lonely." This was the second time the patient had made this request. Miss Forsyth considered such requests encouraging.

"Of course, dear." Ellen smoothed the bedclothes and bathed the clammy face and hands before she sat down beside her.

"Thank you — you are kind," the girl whispered and Ellen felt close to tears at the hopelessness of her low tones.

"Kind?" Ellen asked herself as she looked down at the beautiful stranger. "How could I be anything but kind to one so fragile — so utterly lovely?" And yet she knew that the girl on the bed had been terribly abused and frightened — tortured, perhaps. But why and by whom?

CHAPTER FIVE

IT WAS ON ELLEN's last night in Receiving some ten days before, that the ambulance had been summoned to the lodge of a wealthy broker out on the West Lake Road. The lodge-keeper and his wife, good, honest Irish folk, had been returning on foot from a friend's when a big car passed them at a great rate of speed.

"Liked ta run us down," Barney told Ellen when she talked with the pair while the patient's T.P.R., diagnosis, etc., were being taken in the Receiving Room. "But we thought nothin' of it at th' toime— 'tis a well traveled highway. An' thin when we reached th' lodge gates we see a bundle on th' ground. 'Blankets,' sez I."

"We'll be seein'." Annie Doogan took up the tale. "An glory be t'God! if 'twaren't a body in the blanket—"

" 'Twas only wan, Miss, an' th' pore thing lucked mighty dead t' me."

"I sez t' Barney, sez I: 'I'll fome fer th' ambulance,' sez I, 'an' mebbe th' poleece,' sez I, 'fer 'tis dirty worruk's bin goin' on,' sez I."

"An' I sez. 'Th' ambulance first, Annie darlin','' I sez, 'an' thin mebbe th' poleece,' that's what we done. An' will th' pore thing live, Miss? An' who might she be?"

Ellen could give them no information. There was none to give. The girl — she was, apparently, in her early twenties — was clad only in a cotton wrapper over underwear that had once been elegant. That is, Ellen felt sure their very simplicity and the fineness of the material bespoke a person of good taste and one possessed of a measure of wealth. The wrapper didn't belong. The girl was painfully thin as if from some long illness; but her features — her hands and feet were those of a gentlewoman. In her first faint mutterings, Ellen and Doctor Dent were positive they detected an English accent — hence the title Lady X. There was not a scrap of anything that could be used for identification. Even the shoes — sensible oxfords, while they looked English to Ellen, bore no manufacturer's name or trademark. The wrapper was undoubtedly American and was much too large. The blanket — an automobile robe, was dirty and cheap.

In the sudden emergency, when her life hung by a mere thread, MacGowan had resorted to transfusion. Ellen typed the same, as also did Cyrus Dent. Miss Forsyth grudgingly gave her consent when it was discovered that Ellen had passed her twenty-first birthday a month before. The Superintendent didn't approve of asking her nurses to donate blood — there were professional donors.

"Aye," grunted Angus sourly, "an' there be heather i' th' Hielands an' what of it? It's th' noo — it's th' noo we're needin' blude."

So Ellen had twice given her blood, 500 cc's each time, and young Dent had donated his once, and they both felt an unusual interest in the mystery girl. And for a brief time hostilities ceased.

"Just what relation does that make us, Gaylord?" the young man had asked, grinning at her as they stood beside the patient's narrow bed. "She has your blood and my blood in her veins. She's too old to be our child," he went on audaciously, "but she could be a sort of link between us."

"Isn't it queer how giving a person blood like that seems to create a special feeling for him?" Ellen mused, only half listening to the other. "I wonder who she is— someone important, I'm sure."

"Well, she's got swell blood in her," Cy persisted, "yours and mine. Still dislike me, Gaylord? Even while our good red corpuscles are working happily together inside Lady X, hustling about trying to keep her alive? Aw, Gaylord, I'm not such a bad guy, honestly. Loosen up, gal. Don't be so all-fired Nightingalish."

That last was unfortunate. "I could wish no greater happiness than to be like her," Ellen began with unwonted primness and felt herself a smug little hypocrite. Did she want to be like her entirely? No. No, her heart cried. Florence Nightingale was wonderful — a saint; but Ellen wanted more from life — warmth, love, happiness. A feeling of shame made her angry at herself and at him for producing it.

"God forbid!" she heard Cy say softly. "But of course you don't mean a word of it. No girl as pretty as you are could be satisfied with that kind of a life."

"That's what you think," Ellen snapped, "and what you think isn't in the least important to me."

"Ouch!" cried Cy and clapped his hand to his cheek as if it were something more than a verbal slap, just as Doctor MacGowan entered the room. He eyed the two questioningly. Ellen looked decidedly miffed and the young interne, though grinning, was holding his cheek.

He scowled and Dent vanished. The chief of staff studied the mystery girl's chart and curtly announced the chances of finding her people appeared decidedly hopeless unless the patient regained full consciousness and memory. Ten days had already gone with little if any change. Frowning, he left the ward.

Ann wrinkled her nose at his erect, forbidding back and whispered:

"Angus' corns must be hurting him. Usually he's such a jolly old chap, don't you know. Sometimes I think he hates even himself, Ellen."

"Oh, we all get those days, Ann. But Mac isn't really grouchy — it's just his — his old world physique — his rugged Scotch physiognomy—"

"In other words, he was just born that way — a sourpuss." Ann laughed briefly. She and MacGowan had from the first just naturally antagonized each other. It irked him to work with her and, if possible, he found some excuse for preventing it. Ann knew it and seemed to glory in the fact that she could rile the great Angus." But nae doot his mither lo'ed him— the puir bairn!" Her r's rolled in perfect imitation of Mac's and Ellen laughed. Ann was the limit!

Ellen returned to the end bed. "Comfortable?" she asked as she sat down beside the girl. It was after three and the ward was quiet. Only this one patient was awake.

"Yes," breathed the girl, "quite." Then, after a moment in which her eyes searched Ellen's face, she whispered: "Am—am I going to die?"

"Of course not. You are going to be well and strong again."

"But — but — why am I here? What has happened to me? I—I can't remember. Where am I?" All this scarcely above a whisper; but it was the most she had yet said. Ellen felt a little thrill of excitement.

"You are in Anthony Ware Hospital in Brentwood, New York. You are not to worry or try to think at all. Everything is going to be all right." Ellen spoke slowly and with quiet assurance.

"But — but why am I frightened? Who am I?"

"It will all come back to you when you are stronger," Ellen told her.

"But — but why am I frightened? Who am I?"

"You see, there was an accident and your back and head were injured."

The wide violet eyes lost some of their terror. Ellen smiled and pressed the cold, lifeless hand.

"You are kind," the girl murmured. Her fine brows, oddly dark in one fair, drew together in a frown of perplexity.

"Try to sleep instead of thinking, dear," Ellen urged. "The more you sleep and relax, the sooner you will remember, and we are all going to help you."

"So very kind," she murmured again, and closed her eyes. In a little while she slept that deep trance-like unconsciousness that is own sister to death.

For a long moment Ellen stood looking down at the girl lying so white and still. What lay behind that thick curtain of forgetfulness? And was it possible to build up the broken body and restore the shattered nerves? To pierce the dark veil so that memory would return? She shook her head. Doctor MacGowan had said that eventually, when her bruised and torn back should heal, she would regain the ability to move and if Doctor MacGowan said so it must be true, of that Ellen was certain. He had also said that no doubt her memory would return —at least partially. Sometimes when there had occurred a concussion as serious as Lady X's, memory was never completely restored. Oh, she must get well—she must! Why she was so insistent, Ellen didn't know. Perhaps it was her own blood — demanding to go on living.

Her lips firmed and she slipped from the room and down the length of the long corridor to a great window that looked out upon a suddenly white world. The snow was newly fallen and lay pure and untrampled as far as her eye could reach. She drew back the curtains. Millions of stars glittered in a cold blue-black sky and a slightly lop-sided moon seemed about ready to drop from sight below the horizon of house-tops.

Just like a Christmas card, she thought. Every house on the street was dark. The street lights showed wreaths on a few windows and touched a decorated fir tree or two. Four more days until Christmas. Last year she had been in Pediatrics and what fun they had had! She wondered just what they could do this year to cheer the patients in Ward L.

Doctor Timothy Ware had built and endowed this hospital as a memorial to his father, Anthony Ware, pioneer and philanthropist, and had named the free woman's ward, the Lillian Latham, in memory of his mother. This was shortened to 'Lily,' then to 'Lil' and finally to 'L' — Ward L it remained. A large painting in oils of this same Lilliam Latham, exquisitely beautiful and no doubt idealized, hung between the two long west windows in the ward and on the opposite wall a picture of Christ and the woman taken in adultery.

Ellen always felt antagonistic when she looked at that picture — not because of the subject or the artist's treatment of it; but because it hung in this particular ward. She knew that poverty and sin did not necessarily go hand in hand and she wondered if perhaps that picture was responsible for the attitude of some of the patients here. They were often so terribly snobbish in their poverty. It hurt their pride to be in a free ward at all.

Foolish though no doubt it was, Ellen didn't much blame them, and wished she had the temerity to suggest its removal.

Ann had suggested a tree for Christmas with Doctor Dent acting as Santa Claus; but Miss Forsyth had informed them that Doctor Braddock would impersonate the Christmas saint for the whole hospital, excepting possibly, the private rooms, Male Surgical and L. Ellen could understand omitting private rooms and even Male Surgical, but why L — the charity ward? It seemed to her that of all places in the hospital, L needed cheering most. But, she loyally submitted, no doubt Miss Forsyth had her

41

reasons. She drew the curtains and went back to her table in the alcove. Ann joined her.

"Slavonski's eating oranges again," she said sourly. "At this time of night! There ought to be a law against it and probably there is in any other hospital but this."

"Don't begrudge the poor thing what enjoyment she can get from sucking oranges, Ann," Ellen soothed. "It's little enough pleasure she gets otherwise or ever will in this world."

"But she's so darned selfish with them, Ellen, and I never saw such oranges. Tomorrow I'm going out and buy a half dozen of the biggest I can get and I'm going to eat 'em all. I wish I could do it right in front of her and smack my lips even louder than she does. How long do you suppose she'll be here, Ellen?"

"Until spring, anyway, if not longer. What has she to go back to? One room over a fruit stand with a lazy husband who thinks the government owes him a living. You know she'll probably never walk again, Ann. Why not be nice to her?"

"To her? There you go, Ellen. Be nice to them," she mimicked. "And they run you ragged. Do you know what that Muller woman said to me when I gave her that last drink of water? That she intended giving the Superintendent an earful when she came around next time. Such goings on she never did see. Nurses lazing around, refusing to answer calls and starving them. The food wasn't fit for a dog to eat. Just because she was in a ward didn't mean she wasn't used to good food and proper service. She'd tell her plenty and some of the smart young flibbertigibbets would be losing their easy jobs. Easy jobs! Wish she could follow one of us around for one night — she'd change her tune. Probably endow us with halos."

"I hope you let her rave on and didn't answer, Ann," Ellen said anxiously. "They like to sputter, but they don't really mean anything. She won't complain to Miss Forsyth or to Miss Williams either."

"Oh, won't she? Williams wouldn't listen — she never does. Agatha's different — always looking for lapses. I told her to go on and blab if it would ease her mind any. I didn't care. I don't either."

"Why do you say that, Ann? You do care. And really I think it is probably hard for some of the people in L. Charity is never very easy to accept."

"They ought to be good and thankful they can come here for nothing and be taken care of. No, Ellen, I'm not going to get maudlin over any charity patient. I give them good service and what do I get for it — scowls, black looks and complaints. They're a thankless lot."

"Oh, they're not often like that, Ann —"

"Often enough to make me long to wring their necks even while I sweetly and painstakingly attend to their wants," Ann snapped.

"I think they need something more than service, Ann," Ellen began wistfully, but Ann cut her short.

"I refuse to listen, Ellen. And I had hoped you had outgrown your altruism by this time."

"Oh, well," Ellen laughed, refusing to get into an argument at four in the morning. "Let's talk about our Christmas tree. While you're out tomorrow buying those oranges, you might get some of the things for the tree. There'll be sixteen we know of and probably one or two more — there always are. Better count on twenty. I don't know of any in L who expect to go home for Christmas."

"Count out Slavonski and Muller, Ann said grimly. "They get nothing."

"Oh, Ann!" Ellen protested mildly.

"And where do you get twenty? We've only sixteen beds filled and if Crispi goes home as she insists she will, there'll be only fifteen."

"Crispi won't go home, and it's quite likely all twenty beds will be filled by Christmas, Ann. People seem to fall around more at this time of the year. So really I think we should get a few extra things — one never knows and it would be too bad to miss anyone. We can always take them up front if we have anything over."

"Okay. Here's what I suggest — see what you think of it."

Together they went over the lists — changing an item here and there and adding others.

"I'm flat, Ellen," Ann grumbled. "You'll have to finance the thing. I'll pay you, positively, on the twenty-fourth. Dad always sends me a check."

"Ten dollars ought to cover everything," Ellen figured. "I have a lot of wrappings and seals and things left from my own packages and I snitched three strings of lights from the pile downstairs. Just because this is Ward L, conducted in the name of sweet but cold charity, it doesn't mean that our tree has to be as skimpy and unattractive as most charity it."

Ann laughed. "And I snitched three strings, Ellen, and two boxes of ornaments. Hurrah for our side! Forsyth's a regular Scrooge when it comes to loosening up on decorations. How does she expect us to trim a tree with nothing to use?"

"Do you suppose we can get first pick of the trees when they come, Ann?" Ellen asked. "With six strings of lights, we ought to have a sizable one. I'll go down and select a couple more boxes of doodabs — just nonchalantly, you know — not snitch them this time unless someone questions my right to them. How about getting Dent to pick out a tree for us? He—well—he seems more or less interested in—in—one of our patients here."

Ann hesitated for only a moment. Dent had proven himself a total loss. According to reports, he was out for a girl with social position and money. Only yesterday she had heard of his rushing Sylvia Durston—or she him—one of the Country Club smart young things. Well, let him rush her; from the picture Ann had seen of her in the Sunday paper, she wasn't so much. And what was money? Convenient and necessary to be sure — in a man, but in a girl, youth and beauty, plus that 'certain something,' counted far more. Dent wasn't anything to lose sleep over, anyway. She intended doing much better than a struggling young doctor. The only thing about Dent that had intrigued her was the fact that she couldn't quite make him. That was an unusual thing for her—she always got her man. She had heard he had been attracted to Ellen—had even been attentive to her in a careful, hole-in-a-wall way — trust him to save his cake and eat it, too—the heel! Well, she was sure Ellen wouldn't fall for him — he was too sure of himself, too nonchalant and smooth, and Ellen was set on following through to a medical career—the poor, willfully blind imbecile!

44

"Okay! We'll get the pick of the lot or my fatal charm is losing its potency," she promised flippantly. "Did you know Forsyth has the sentimental idea we should sing carols on Christmas Eve? Imagine! I can't carry a tune across the street — no ear for music at all. I suggested you do the singing, Ellen, but Agatha frowned on it. The old pill! Just because I thought of it first. And yet you're the only one of the gang with a real voice."

Ellen laughed. She was entirely familiar with the Superintendent's determination to manage things in her own way. She might ask for suggestions — criticisms even; but in the more than two years of Ellen's association with her, she had not known of Miss Forsyth adopting one suggestion or accepting one bit of criticism, no matter how constructive either might be. Miss Williams, the Night Superintendent, and she got along beautifully because Hattie Williams kept her ideas to herself. But in spite of this, Ellen liked Miss Forsyth—liked and admired her.

"Oh, well, what does it matter, Ann? I love carol singing and I didn't think she would allow it. I wonder why she thought of it this year."

"Nitwit!" Ann jeered. "Haven't you tumbled to the fact she's soft on Braddock? Braddock mentioned the fact that down in the Missus' home town, carols were sung at Christmas time and this year she had mentioned that she missed them. The old girl is failing, they tell me. Really getting ready to pass in her checks at last so it's no particular strain on Agatha's part to donate our services to make her happy — or at least less miserable. Do you mean to say you didn't know she was soft on him?"

"Oh, you! You're soft in the head, Ann," Ellen spoke without rancor and Ann wasn't in the least offended. "You know, Ann," Ellen went on, "Christmas just naturally seems to call for carols."

Ann wasn't so sure. As she said, she had no ear for music and had difficulty in following a tune; but Ellen assured her she would lend physical if not vocal beauty to any group and Ann's interest quickened, then sagged.

"But we'll be on duty, Ellen. How can we sing carols?"

"We can't; but that doesn't alter the fact that we ought

to have carols on Christmas Eve. We can listen, can't we? I'm all for it."

"Listen? 'Way back here? Probably can't hear a note. Oh, I don't care, Ellen. You sing to the ward— they'll love it."

The hospital was awakening. Not noisily, but with the subdued hum of a giant beehive. Lights flashed oftener; the elevators swished up and down; telephones rang and from the courtyard below, truck brakes squealed and the siren of the ambulance shrilled as it reached the street. Ann yawned and stretched. Ellen straightened the table and went down the yard for a final inspection before she should go off duty.

With the exception of one or two, the ward was asleep. Ellen paused beside Lady X. Did she look a little less waxen? She felt her pulse, smiled and added a note to her chart. Another night had gone to join its millions of brothers. This one had been without incident and like most quiet, uneventful nights, had been a little trying. Ellen looked forward gratefully to the luxury of a warm bath and bed.

CHAPTER SIX

THE TREE WAS up in Ward L — a shapely spruce. Doctor Dent and an orderly had placed it at one end of the long room—the end nearest the bed of Lady X. Hospital discipline had relaxed somewhat. Ann and Ellen brought their gayly wrapped packages while the day staff was still on duty and the four girls worked swiftly. At first the mystery girl had shown little interest in the unusual activity going on about her; but when the nurses began hanging the gay decorations and strings of colored lights, the wide, violet eyes glistened.

The whole ward watched—even Mrs. Slavonski, who had been sullen for hours, brightened, and Mrs. Nolan, the latest fractured hip case, forgot for a moment the excruciating pain and the discomfort of her inactivity, and joined with the others in offering suggestions and comments, some of which were, to say the least, decidedly frank.

Angela Dubail, the little diabetic-heart case, wore her perpetual smile, her dark eyes purple-rimmed and inordinately brilliant. She lay with her rosary-entwined hands clasped on her childishly flat breast and watched, wanting nothing. She never wanted anything. Ellen wished she would. She yearned over her in a way that aroused Ann's ire. The girl would be better out of her misery and free from her beast of a husband. Ellen knew that probably Ann was right, but her heart ached every time she came near the bed. She wondered if the girl sensed her tender pity, for her eyes would glow with some inner light and the smile that greeted her was poignantly sweet. So young to die as die she must. Ellen, who had seen death come in so many different guises since that Christmas Eve when little Eloise had gratefully slipped away, no longer looked upon it as always an enemy. Sometimes it was indeed a friend—leading one into another, pleasanter room — to the beginning of another and grander adventure. Oh, there were so many worse things than death; so much that was far harder to bear!

Mrs. Crispi had ceased her everlasting moaning at her failure to leave and thought the star that graced the top of the tree far too small and not very bright, either.

Couldn't someone go out to her place and get one of the kids to lend them theirs? They'd much rather have "a pitcher of Roosevelt on it anyways—swell Americans, they was." But the star stayed put and all by Mrs. Crispi thought it absolutely lovely.

The ward was childishly jubilant. At five o'clock Doctor MacGowan and Miss Forsyth, followed by the House Physician and the two internes, stopped in on their tour of inspection through the hospital, and Ellen held her breath. The other nurses were merely attentively respectful.

"Best of the lot!" the Chief of Staff said heartily.

Miss Forsyth eyed the tree somewhat belligerently, her eyes suspicious. Doctor Braddock grinned at Ellen and Dent looked blandly innocent.

"You have a great many lights, it seems to me," the Superintendent said and Ellen was sure she was counting each glowing bulb. "How is it you have so many? They were to be proportioned." She looked coldly at the girls, two of whom were perfectly innocent as to just where the lights in question had come from. Ann looked hurt at even the suggestion of greediness. No one said anything.

"Well, you see, Miss Forsyth—" Ellen began.

"A tree of this size needs plenty of lights," Doctor MacGowan interposed crisply. "One less would spoil it."

"But—but—in the reception rooms—"

"Umph!" the surgeon growled. "Where else would they be so much appreciated as right here in Ward L?"

"Why, he's splendid!" Something of her unspoken admiration showed in Ellen's brown eyes, for the stern, ugly face of the surgeon broke into a rare and unexpected smile.

Cyrus Dent silently clapped his hands and again the plump little House Physician grinned at Ellen. What a grand bunch they were, she thought, her heart warming to them. The chief hadn't finished.

"You're doing a fine job, Gaylord, and I'm not referring wholly to the tree. Some time I want to have a talk with you about our mysterious guest."

Ellen glowed with pleasure. He had scarcely noticed her before. Even when she was privileged to assist him she felt that she had been just someone to stand silently by, anticipating his needs with quick intelligence and skilful hands. She had even thought him quite unaware of her identity.

Miss Forsyth stiffened and the eyes and mouths of the others showed signs of opening in amazement. Angus unbending! Angus noticing a girl! Would wonders never cease?

"Thank you, Doctor," Ellen murmured, "any time you ·ish."

Her back stiff with disapproval, the Superintendent ·ollowed the surgeon from the room. Doctor Braddock, still smiling, was close behind and the two young internes tip-toed after in exaggerated stealth. Ann Murdock braced herself, her fists clenched, her expression pugnacious.

"I like that! Say, who did most of the dirty work on this tree, anyway?"

"I did!" chorused the other three.

"You did not. I did. I wrangled Cy Dent into snitching the best one for us, didn't I?"

"Call that dirty work?" Frances Blaine asked, quizzical eyes on Ellen. "Dent would sure be flattered to hear that, wouldn't he, Gaylord?"

"Oh, forget it, Ann," pleaded Ellen, eager to keep the peace, "and come on over to the house. We haven't too much time to change before dinner. Thanks, girls. We should have been lost without you."

"Like fun, we should," muttered Ann.

"What's the matter with you?" Ellen asked as they walked the short distance to the Nurses' Home. "You've been touchy all afternoon."

"You'd be touchy, too, if you had got word that your best friend had put one over on you."

"What do you mean? How, put one over?"

"Got herself engaged to the man I've been in love with all my life. And has the colossal nerve to write me that she knows I'll be happy about it because Tip and I have always been so keen about each other. If that isn't crowding the mourners, I don't know what you'd call it."

Ellen smiled. This was the first time she had heard of Ann's great, deathless love. Ann was always going through some dramatic experience — some crisis in her life. She gave her companion a little push.

"Snap out of it! You're no more in love with this Tip than I am. Why, Ann, you don't know what being in love means."

"Is that so?" snapped Ann. "And I suppose you do?"

Ellen was surprised and annoyed to feel herself reddening. Of course she didn't.

"Ye-ah!" Ann went on bitterly, deaf to the other's silence. "Just a little sister of healing — a sweet, sympathetic Florence Nightingale! Wonderful! Only I bᵉ' you hate nursing as much as the rest of us do. Don't tell me you're satisfied to take care of a bunch of disgustingly selfish sick people all your life, Ellen Gaylord, for I won't believe it."

"But it's true, Ann. You know I'm keen about my work. I wish I had money enough to go on and study to become a doctor, but I—I can't—right now." Ellen's voice was quietly sincere. "I'm proud and happy I'm a nurse."

"You're welcome to it, Ann muttered, but some of the angry hurt went out of her voice. She linked her arm in Ellen's. "Fine Christmas spirit I have—of the Scrooge variety," she mocked. "Oh, well, I ought to have known that absence ever makes the heart grow fonder of the other gal. Only, I hope they have quintuplets the first year—darn them!" Suddenly, she began to laugh, at first shrilly, then somewhat tearfully. She stifled a sob. "Life's a mess, Ellen. You see, I—I really do like Tip—rather a lot!"

"Oh, Ann, I'm sorry!" Ellen said softly, and gave her a quick little hug of sympathy. "Is there anything I can do to help?"

"N-not a thing—but—but thanks for being sorry." She was trying hard to keep from weeping openly and when she reached her room she went in and shut the door. Ellen stood for a moment uncertain what to do. Ann would hate anyone seeing her break down — weep. Better to let her thrash it out by herself, then no one could pity her—Ann hated pity. Poor Ann! Was she truly hurt in her heart, or was it just her pride that suffered?

Ellen slipped into a clean uniform and stood for a moment contemplating the packages on her dressing table. All of them bore the legend "Not To Be Opened Until Christmas" or some similar admonition. She went to her closet and collected an armful of gayly wrapped gifts. She would distribute them now, before dinner. They were simple gifts—not one of them costly; a handmade handkerchief, a corsage of ribbon flowers, sweet-smelling sachets, gayly decorated hangers. The salaries of the graduate nurses at Anthony Ware had never been large and just lately had been pared even more. The student nurses received no compensation whatever, and there was not a wealthy girl in the house, so gifts were of neccessity inexpensive. But as she deposited the last package, Ellen murmured:

"They're peaches, every one of them, and the hospitals should be proud of them."

As a matter of fact, the hospital was proud of its staff and except for an occasional infringement of its somewhat rigid rules which were, with reservations, strictly enforced and, also with reservations, almost as strictly adhered to, there was little if any serious complaining. Ann, of course, was a law unto herself and remained so quite miraculously, throughout her years of training. Each entering class of probationers was hand-picked and carefully tested during the three month period before acceptance. Its training school rated high in the profession and to be known as an Anthony Ware graduate meant superiority-plus.

Ellen wondered if Ann would be down to dinner but she was already in the dining-room when Ellen entered and except for an excess of color in her cheeks and slightly shadowed eyes, she showed no signs of heartbreak. Ellen was relieved. Her smile was returned by a wry twisting of Ann's lips.

Dinner that night was a gala affair. Mrs. Drake, the House Mother and Ella Poole, the Dietitian, had planned an elaborate menu. A two-foot tree centered the long table and red candles in graduating heights marched in single file down opposite sides of the brightly lighted centerpiece. At each place was a red basket filled with home made candies and a spray of holly lay on each snowy napkin. As they found their places, the nurses stood and cheered the perpetrators and were not in the least surprised when the two young internes appeared in the doorway begging admission.

"Go back to your own celebration," Mrs. Drake ordered them severely. "We can't disarrange the table at this late date."

"Heck!" young Fielding cried. "Know who's dining over there? The President of the Board —old Hatchet-face! Doc. Angus MacGowan—our dour Scottie—God bless him! An ancient dame by the name of Ware—bad cess to her! And our own beloved, merry-hearted Agatha! Save us, girls! Have a heart! Where's your boasted Christmas spirit? Where's—"

Cyrus Dent tried to hush him but it was too late. Suddenly behind them loomed an austere and awe-inspiring quartette. Miss Forsyth and Doctor MacGowan must certainly have heard. Young Fielding tried desperately to make himself invisible.

The twenty or more nurses stood motionless behind their chairs. Their faces were flushed in an effort to suppress their mirth—their eyes straight ahead.

"I want you to see the happy arrangements we have made for the pleasure of our Staff at this joyous Christmas season, ladies," Miss Forsyth said smoothly, her eyes boring into the reddened neck of the talkative interne. "Miss Ware, I'm sure your grandfather would have approved. Records show how much he endeavored to make his Staff feel at ease and like one big happy family." Her icy glance passed over the two young men. "Of course, these young men are mere on-lookers like ourselves. We still hold to the old traditions—absolutely no friendly relations between male and female members of our Staff. I see you agree, Miss Ware— Mrs. Preston?" as the old ladies nodded vigorously, one of Miss Ware's thin, be-ringed hands cupping an ear. "Our dinner is being served in the dining-room of my suite." She summoned a smile to include the surgeon and her two guests. "Charming picture, don't you agree?" then turned and ushered the two old ladies out.

Doctor MacGowan lingered for a moment, his face wearing its usual granite mask. Fielding and Dent stood like two bad boys awaiting a well-merited punishment. Ellen knew a wild desire to laugh. She felt it well up inside her and threaten imminent disgrace. She swallowed hard and caught Ann's exaggeratedly bland stare. That was too much. She choked, and as if a spring had been released, a shout of laughter went up from the girls around the table. Mrs. Burke and Miss Poole vanished into the kitchen. Fielding tried to sneak past the tall angular surgeon, but he barred the way.

"Thanks for the invocation, er—Fielding," Doctor MacGowan rumbled, deep in his throat. "I hope the Almighty heard you." He bowed to the demoralized nurses. "A merry Christmas to you, young ladies, and may you enjoy your dinner without further interruption. Come along, my dear-r-r sir-r-rs, our own—er—beloved, merry-hearted company awaits us."

Came a breathless stillness as the door closed on the trio. The girls sank into their chair and leaned back —helpless.

"Would one have believed Doctor MacGowan had a sense of humor?" Ellen asked in surprise as she wiped her eyes.

"Ye-ah," Ann scoffed. "The same brand of humor an inquisitor enjoyed when he shouted 'off with his head!' I bet those two lads wish they were somewhere else."

"Oh, well, they had it coming to them," someone said as she dipped into her soup.

The dinner was prolonged and hilarious. The girls lingered until a message arrived from Miss Forsyth reminding those who were to sing carols that the time was growing short. She was desirous her distinguished guests should hear them.

Seven-thirty and the night force was back on duty, relieving the skeleton staff who went down thankfully to their own specially prepared dinner. The hospital settled down to its usual night routine. Eight, and the singing began. Visitors went to windows. Patients in private rooms begged that doors and windows be left slightly ajar. Lips smiled that so recently had been twisted in pain and would be all too soon again. Thoughts traveled back over the years to other Christmases. Patients and callers, doctors and nurses on duty, joined in the singing.

Back in Ward L, high up in the rear of the hospital, the sound came but faintly and Ellen sang the first carol with them.

> "Holy night—peaceful night
> All is calm—all is bright
> Round yon Virgin, Mother and Child,
> Holy infant so tender and mild
> Sleep in heavenly pe-eace—
> Sleep in heavenly peace."

Mrs Slavonski, from her bed at the far end of the ward, called to Ann.

"My man—he giff me more oranges. Beeg bag off them." She reached beneath the bedclothes and motioned for Ann to pull them out.

"But—but—you know, Mrs.—" began Ann. Selfish old thing! No soul at all. Eat-eat-eat, while Ellen sang like an angel.

"You giff them—all off them. You nice gurls. Take." She shut her eyes as if the sight was more than she could bear. "Hurry! Take! Giff—giff!"

The bag was heavy but Ann carried it to Ellen. "Well," she cried as she dumped them on the table before her, "the Christmas spirit has caught Slavonski squarely in her stomach! Two dozen, Ellen!"

"Enough for the whole Ward and some for the young-sters in Pediatrics! Good for Slavonski!" applauded Ellen. she went down to the swarthy old woman who was in all probability never to walk again, and told her how happy she had made them.

" 'Sall right, Miss Nurse. My man, he breeng 'em— for Crissmas gif' to 'ospital 'ere."

"He did? That was grand of him. You tell him how grateful we are, won't you?"

The wrinkled brown face on the pillow puckered in a frown of sorrow and disappointment.

"He breeng me notting—notting a-tall. He peeg!" She spit out the last venomously, then sobbed once, retch-ingly, tears streaming down her leathery cheeks.

"Oh no, Mrs. Slavonski. Tomorrow is Christmas. He'll be here bright and early in the morning to see you and to bring you something. You'll see." She bent and whispered softly. "Anyway, Santa Claus left something on the tree for you."

"Non—non—not for me?" The old face twisted painfully.

"You just wait and see. You're going to have a grand Christmas!"

"I'll get hold of Tony and see that old Slavonski brings her something tomorrow if he has to bind and gag him and if I have to pay for it myself," Ellen vowed as she went on down the ward.

"I remember a tree like that, Nurse," Lady X whispered when Ellen stopped at her bed. "Only there were candles on it and I have heard that carol you sang just now. Will you sing it again, please? Just for me?" And Ellen sang softly, there close to the bed of the mystery girl. The pale lips moved and Ellen knew she was singing with her, though no sound came. The deep violet eyes were flooded with tears.

"Oh, why cannot I remember?" she whispered.

"You will, all in good time. Just relax and don't try to think. I'm sure you are going to have a lovely Christmas. Santa Claus left something on the tree for everyone. So, close your eyes and go right to sleep—" she urged smilingly, "morning will come that much quicker if you do."

"You are so kind," the girl whispered. "Everyone is so kind." A shadow flitted across her face and was gone.

Everyone wasn't always kind, Ellen knew. She wondered how much longer it would be before recollection came. She wondered, too, if perhaps Doctor Dent had joined the carol singers. They were over now. The last visitors gone. The hospital had settled down for the night. Ann had wandered over to Maternity to see the twins, born that morning to the wife of the town's Chief of Police. The elevator whirred and Ellen's heart missed a beat. But it was only Joe Chilson, the night watchman, come to fix a shutter that was loose.

Ellen called herself an idiot. Cy Dent was no doubt spending Christmas Eve with some of Brentwood's gay young people. He was one of the most popular men ever to interne in Anthony Ware. A feeling of desolation swept over her for a moment and she longed for home. Eleven o'clock — the tree was probably all trimmed now and Dad and Mother and the grandchildren were in bed; but she visioned her sisters and brothers and in-laws sitting down to a snack of sandwiches and coffee or maybe griddlecakes and maple syrup with little home-made sausages. Her eyes filled. What wouldn't she give for just one little peek into that big, warm old kitchen! The hospital corridor was lonely tonight; the wind howled dismally as it swept around the corner of the ancient building. Even the mystery girl was asleep —all the world was asleep she felt—asleep or having a good time somewhere. Mentally, she shook herself. What ailed her? This was no way to feel on Christmas Eve.

"Holy night—peaceful night—
All is calm—all is bright—"
she hummed softly and felt comforted.

Down in MacGowan's office, Cyrus Dent and the Chief of Staff were discussing Lady X's condition. At last the older man got wearily to his feet. It had been a hard day—a long day.

"Aye, she's stronger. I'm sure o' that. And in time nae doot she'll recall her name. We maun na be impatient, lad. Just bide a bit." He opened the door— touched the young man's shoulder as he went out. "Gude night, Doctor."

"Not be impatient!" muttered Cy as he left the hospital. "I've a hunch my plan'll hurry things along a bit. Time! Wait! Too much time has been lost already. We've waited long enough. Action is indicated."

He swung down the snowy street, humming softly:
"Holy night—peaceful night—
All is calm—all is bright—"
Nightingale would be relieved to discover the identity of Lady X, he was sure of that. If his plan worked—it just had to work!

CHAPTER SEVEN

"Cast your eyes on this blurb, Gaylord." Cyrus Dent laid a folded newspaper on the table in the corridor of Ward L and thrust thumbs through imaginary suspenders.

"WHO IS LADY X?" (Ellen read)
"An interesting case of amnesia is under observation at Anthony Ware Hospital. Some two weeks ago, the patient, a beautiful and, apparently, well bred girl of about twenty, was found in an unconscious condition near the lodge of T. Montgomery Davis, on West Lake Road.

"At the hospital it was discovered she was suffering head and spine injuries causing complete though, perhaps, temporary paralysis.

"There is no slightest clue to her identity aside from the fact that she is probably English, hence the title given her by the hospital staff.

"Lady X is five feet two inches tall, has shoulder length golden blonde hair, large eyes of a particularly deep shade of violet, perfect teeth; is small boned with slender hands and feet.

"THE DAILY HERALD will appreciate information that might lead to the discovery of any relative or friend of the unfortunate young lady.

"Address all communications to
Editor THE DAILY HERALD
Brentwood, New York."

"Did you do this, Doctor?" Ellen asked and at his nod of assent, "Does Doctor MacGowan know, and Miss Forsyth?"

"Sure, they know, and was I surprised to find that Mac had sent this same description to London on the strength of our hunch she was English! Something is bound to break soon. A girl like her just can't drop out without leaving a ripple."

"I'm not so sure of that," Ellen demurred. "People are always disappearing and never being heard from. And did you stop to think, Doctor Dent, what this publicity might do? That is might endanger her life again?'

"How, for Pete's sake?"

"We-ll, those beasts who threw her from that car probably thought she was dead or dying and when they discover she isn't—didn't—"

"They wouldn't dare!" Dent cried, but Ellen saw that he was impressed. "I'll take that point up with Mac, and we'll be on our guard." He shrugged. "Whoever heard of a holdup in Brentwood? This burg is only half alive."

"Just the same, I'm glad she's in a ward. Fifteen or twenty fellow patients and a couple of husky nurses ought to provide ample protection."

Cyrus Dent grinned at Ann Murdock who was, presumably, studying nearby; at least, she had a text book in her hand. "We're just a couple of old grannies, Gaylord. We act as if Lady X was our problem child."

Ann's lip curled. "It's fortunate for the girl that she has looks," she said cynically. "Problem cases aren't popular as a rule."

Ellen's eyes were clouded as she shook her head. "Lady X was never a problem child. I'll wager she was always sweet and lovely. Oh, I wish she could remember something—anything! It's all so terribly hopeless—like —like fighting an invisible enemy."

"Calm yourself, darling!" murmured Ann, and Doctor Dent said:

"Give her time, Gaylord. Mac says she's distinctly on the mend. She'll snap out of it, perhaps suddenly. Maybe something will happen to pierce that black veil. We've just got to keep on waiting." Actually, he had a hunch it wouldn't be long, now.

Ann made a sound that brought a glare of antagonism from him. He turned sharply and strode down the hall toward the staircase as the soft whirr of the ascending elevator announced the probable arrival of the midnight sandwiches and coffee.

But it was not food that arrived and it was well that Dent had disappeared around the corner, for the tall, angular figure of the Chief of Staff left the elevator and approached the alcove. Ann slipped through the nearest door. Ellen caught her breath. Dent certainly was lucky. Perhaps they were all lucky.

Doctor MacGowan was in hospital white. No doubt some emergency operation. Ellen stood to receive him, but he motioned her to sit and seated himself on the table where he toyed with the charts upon which Ellen had been working.

"About the girl in there, Gaylord," he began without preamble. "She's quite apt to recover her memory any time now." He paused and studied her for a moment. "She seems to cling to you and I wish you would spend as much time with her as is possible. Miss Forsyth is assigning Holmes to your job temporarily and we are moving—er—" his mouth twitched slightly, "Lady X to a private room tomorrow morning."

"Oh, I'm sorry, Doctor MacGowan," Ellen said impulsively, her anxiety overcoming her awe of the great man and making her forget for the moment that a nurse, especially a student nurse, obeys the doctor unquestioningly no matter what the circumstances. "Somehow, I feel she is safer here —in a ward."

"Safer?" the surgeon echoed, astonished.

"Yes. How do we know what those wretches will attempt when they know she isn't dead? They must know—realize she will talk—tell what she knows when her memory returns."

"I see. You think it was the work of gangsters, perhaps?" His eyes twinkled for a moment. "Then you believe the Doogans' wild tale of a speeding car full of desperados? Remember, this is Brentwood."

"I know; but I certainly believe she has been terribly abused—perhaps tortured—by someone. And who but gangsters would be capable of doing such atrocious things? Her poor body was a mass of bruises and her eyes haven't yet lost their look of terror."

The surgeon thoughtfully and painstakingly made a pile of the charts on the table beside him, matching the corners carefully, then suddenly spreading them fanwise.

"The London police are working on the case, also the police in New York. It seems almost hopeless unless she remembers her name. If and when she does, we can go after them." His rather bleak gray eyes searched her face, but the girl was too preoccupied to notice, and even his next remark failed to make her self-conscious. "Doctor Dent is interesting himself in her affairs."

"Yes, I know." Ellen smiled up at the ugly, clever face above her. "I'm glad, for it must grow rather monotonous here to young men like Doctor Dent and Doctor Fielding."

"I suppose so, though I doubt if Dent finds life in Anthony Ware exactly tiresome. At least, he shouldn't," he muttered the last.

Ellen hastened to correct her statement. "I meant that Anthony Ware is small and Brentwood is just a big Country town—"

"I know, Gaylord—" the surgeon interrupted, "but life is much the same all over. The panorama of birth and death disease and accident unrolls here just as it does in larger cities, though, of course on a smaller scale. Our internes and other staff members receive excellent training—fine experience. Some of the world's greatest scientists, doctors and surgeons, hold clinics and give lectures here. Anthony Ware provided for that when he endowed the place. I know that I have spent profitable years in this hospital. I shall take with me to Edinburgh much that will be helpful to my colleagues there when I begin my sabbatical in August." Then, abruptly. "Are you happy here, child?"

It was a long speech—a friendly, intimate recital, and Ellen listened in a daze. Could this be the forebidding MacGowan of whom they all stood in awe? Why, he was fascinating! His ugly face was actually attractive! How had she ever thought his eyes cold and repellent or his mouth more than a little cynical?

"Perfectly happy, Doctor MacGowan. I love nursing. I am doing just what I planned to do when I was a tiny girl, only—well—in my dreams, I went farther—"

"Farther? You mean you dreamed of becoming a doctor?"

"Yes, Doctor MacGowan; but I'm afraid that is out, at least for a time."

"Good! I have long regretted, comparatively, there are so few good woman doctors. Nurses, yes and a fine band of women they are; but I wish some of them would go on."

Ellen stared. Imagine a dominant male willing to welcome a woman within the sacred precincts of his profession! Before she could express her surprise and gratification, he said,

with what Ellen thought was, for him, amazing camara-
derie:

"I hear good reports of you, Gaylord. You are a credit
to your profession and to Anthony Ware. I hope you will
completely realize your ambition, but perhaps becoming a
doctor's wife wouldn't be amiss. A man could go far had
he a lass like you at hame keeping warm his hearthstone."

Ellen's eyes widened in startled surprise. She must be
dreaming. This couldn't be the man before whose black
frown, cold gray eyes and icy, caustic speech, she and the
rest of the staff grew awkward and stiff with dread!

"Why—why, Doctor MacGowan, you're young—" she
began, then blushed scarlet at her gaucherie.

The gray eyes twinkled again. "What did you think?"
he asked whimsically. "I'm thirty-six. Not a great age but
not exactly juvenile either. But come, tell me something
about yourself. This is not your home town?"

Would wonders never cease? From just beyond the door
opposite, Ellen could see Ann Murdock gesticulating. Hand
on heart she pretended to faint. She fanned herself. She
made frightful grimaces. Ellen turned her shoulder and
tried to keep her answer cool and sensible.

"No, Doctor MacGowan. My home is in Michigan. My
people are farmers—have been for generations, though not
always in Michigan. I have two brothers and two sisters, all
married and living near home. I'm the youngest." She
smiled up at him and felt Ann's piercing stare. "There's
nothing extraordinary about me, you see."

"You came a long way to train, didn't you?" he asked.

"Yes, but you see, my Aunt Bess persuaded Mother and
Dad to let me come here. Her husband was Doctor John
Gaylord. He was once on the staff of Anthony Ware and
Aunt Bess has always had an interest in the place."

"Does she live in town?"

"Not now. Since Uncle John died she has spent all her
time in what used to be their summer home on Lake On-
tario, a couple of miles from Deacon's Landing. Deacon's
Landing is just a small station—really just a stop—with
perhaps ten or a dozen houses scattered about. I spend my
rest periods there. It's lovely, even in winter."

"And you finish in June? Then what?" he asked.

Ellen felt the blood rush hotly to her cheeks. Had Mac

heard anything about Cy Dent's attentions to her and misunderstood? But surely they were slight and had ceased altogether now. She stole a glance at the surgeon but he was intent on matching the corners of the charts and his expression was entirely free from guile.

"Private duty, I suppose," she said. "My people hope I shall soon be nearer home."

"And you?"

"I like the East, but I imagine I shall go home for a while. Our family doctor says he can keep me busy if I decide to stay out there."

His eyes searched her face for a moment, but Ellen was once more entirely serene. "I see," he murmured. "Thank you. Now about our mysterious guest—perhaps we shall leave her where she is for a few days longer. In the meantime, we may hear from some interested party." He stood up, tall, ungainly and grim once more. He didn't use the elevator, but disappeared around the corner of the corridor where the stairs were.

Ann Murdock crept to the door, poked her head out then came stealthily nearer, her eyes and mouth round with surprise and mockery.

"Have a care, me less!" she warned. "If Agatha gets wise to these rendezvous, it'll be just too bad for 'teacher's pet.' What did the Maharajah of Indoors want, anyway?"

"Oh, nothing much," Ellen assured her, still in something of a daze. "It's Lady X who's the cause of my sudden popularity, Ann. Mac seems to think her memory is about due to return."

"So what?"

"So nothing, except we'll know who she is and shall be able to prosecute the beasts who—"

"Calm yourself, sweeheart," Ann interrupted callously. "How do you know she's not a moll? You and Dent are positively gaga over that girl. Be careful, precious, she doesn't cut you out. Nothing like a bit of mystery together with a touch of wide-eyed innocence to ensnare the wariest of males, especially if she turns out to be really someone—as you both insist she is. They do say our Cy's out for big game—well heeled."

"For heaven's sake, Ann!" Ellen cried, exasperated. "Haven't you a thought above—"

"Sure I have," Ann interrupted, unperturbed. "But I hate seeing you deliberately throwing away your chances—I understand you have, or once had, chances. After all, Dent's probably going places and he's more or less—er—the best bet this dump has had in a coon's age. I've no doubt you could land him even yet, if you tried. He seems still to sort of haunt your locality, I've noticed. I thought, perhaps, that was why Angus ducked up here right after Cy ducked down—to sort of warn you to use discretion in your affair or, on the other hand, to give you his blessing" A sudden thought seemed to strike her. "Sa-ay—Angus isn't by any chance—you aren't two-timing Cy, are you? He's still—well —sort of—"

"And suppose he is—or was—sort of—? What has that to do with our interest in Lady X? I tell you, Ann, that girl is someone important and I don't blame Doctor Dent for being a bit maudlin over her—as you insist he is. I confess I am myself and so is Mac—"

"It couldn't be the Maharajah himself who has the inside track, could it?" Ann went on as if Ellen hadn't spoken. "They do say the Chief is quite a man in the surgical world. Perhaps you're wise to hitch your hope-chest to a sur—"

Ellen was really angry. Her brown eyes flashed. "Ann Murdock," she snapped, her voice quiet but distinct, "what ails you? Are you crazy? Listen! You will kindly leave me out of your stupid match-making plans from now on. I don't want to hear another word about it. Understand? I'm not interested. I mean it."

"Sorry, sweetheart," Ann replied, quite unimpressed, "but I wish I had your chances. I don't know but—" The whirring of the elevator as it started on its last lap upward, hastened the ending of her sentence. "—perhaps you're wise to favor Scotty. After all, Dent's scarcely dry behind the ears and Angus—what a man! Food!"

She left Ellen fuming impotently, and strode down the corridor to meet Marcella Harris.

CHAPTER EIGHT

MARCELLA HARRIS POKED her head into Ellen's room soon after two o'clock that afternoon on the chance that Ellen might be awake. Ellen was. Much to the girl's annoyance, Ann's persistent talk about men and marriage kept recurring and followed fantastically into her dreams. She lay now, wondering just how much, if any, of Ann's nonsense had even a grain of truth in it. Lady X was lovely, even in her emaciated condition. Her eyes did brighten when Cy came into the ward—Ellen had noticed and rejoiced this very night at the awakening of her interest in people. And no matter how ritzy Lady X proved to be, she could do much worse than marry a rising young doctor. In Ellen's opinion there could be no grander life for a girl no matter what her station, than to marry an ambitious young man and match her step with his on his climb to success, if, of course, matrimony was her goal. Unconsciously, Ellen sighed. Why, she couldn't imagine, for she wasn't the least bit unhappy in the thought that her own goal when reached meant a lifetime of hardship, sacrifice and probable loneliness.

The thin, ugly yet attractive face of Doctor MacGowan crowded young Dent out. Ellen found her heartbeat quickening. What a surprise the man had proved to be! Imagine going to Scotland with him!

"Ellen Gaylord, you're the world's prize idiot!" she scolded herself. "You've been bitten by the same bug that's making Ann impossible. MacGowan wouldn't look at you that way and even if he did, you couldn't possibly fall for him and you know it. You have ambitions, my girl, I know; but you'd never marry a man just to satisfy them. Better leave such things to Ann Murdock and her kind."

"It's a grand afternoon, Ellen," Marcella said as she came into the room. "Let's go to a matinee and have dinner downtown. I feel like a spree and I have a ten-spot burning a hole in my pocket."

"Thank you, Marcy; but I promised myself I'd go skating this afternoon. I was over at the park on Sunday and the ice is wonderful. Come with me. The air will do you good—more good than sitting in a theatre. The dinner appeals to me, but I'm out of sorts. I want to go off by myself and meditate or maybe just sulk. I'd be poor company for you, darling, but thank you all the same."

"Okay," Marcella said good-naturedly. "Some other time. I feel in the mood for a slinky society play with a wholly indigestible dinner after it. S'long. See you in church—some time."

Ellen donned skiing pants and a warm plaid Machinaw and started for the little park on the outskirts of Brentwood. Head up, eyes straight ahead, she strode along, skates across her shoulders, arms swinging rhythmically, thoughts still chaotic. No doubt it was foolish of her to be angry with Ann. Ann had always been frivolous and meddlesome and Ellen had never ceased wondering that she had chosen nursing of all professions, and yet Ann was a very good nurse. No doubt it was as Ann had said, the hospital provided board and lodging and there was always the chance of a wealthy patient falling in love with his nurse or, perhaps, a doctor—not just any doctor, but a specialist, losing his heart to her. Ann knew her own decorative value and felt it was worth a trial, especially as there was always Tip Waring in the background if she couldn't do better. Now, apparently, Tip had grown tired of waiting. Why didn't Ann stick to the planning of her own future instead of trying to mess up Ellen's life?

Snow crunched under her feet, the air was stimulating—like cold, spiced wine. Her blood tingled. She quickened her pace. In a little while the lake would be crowded with school children and she felt that she needed quiet. A voice hailed:

"Out for the Olympics, Nightingale?"

Ellen swung around. Cyrus Dent fell into step and lifted her skates to his own shoulder. Pointedly, Ellen said nothing.

"Two minds with but a single thought—or words to that effect. Ever stop to think how we enjoy the same things—have the same tastes? In other words, sort of suit each other? Ouch! That one went foul," as Ellen's eyes flashed dangerously. "I mean, we sort of feel the same way about things. Take this for instance. I felt sort of low in my mind today and thought that a dose of fresh air on ice was indicated. You felt the same way, no doubt—though probably being you, you didn't happen to be low in your mind—if any." He chuckled and turned a teasing glance her way. Ellen was walking fast, eyes front, chin slightly elevated, mouth grim. "I meant to ask you last night to forget your horrible habit of obeying cruel and inhuman rules and give me a date; but we were interrupted. Why is it that someone always feels it his duty to butt in on our rendezvous?"

Ellen gasped. How dare he? Doctor Dent went on as if he had not heard that gasp. He wondered just why Ellen gave such a fillip to his life at Anthony Ware. An imp of mischief seemed to take possession of him when he was with her and made him do and say the outlandish things he knew would bring an angry flush to her cheeks and a gleam to her usually placid and, he thought for a young and beautiful girl, too serene brown eyes.

"Let's take the farther entrance—less apt to meet people we know—more privacy."

"Privacy it what I came out for," Ellen said shortly and instantly regretted it. How silly to let him think he had the power to annoy her! If Ann hadn't put a lot of foolish ideas into her head maybe she wouldn't have felt so edgy this afternoon. After all, she and Doctor Dent had to meet from time to time although she avoided him (not too successfully) whenever possible. But they were both interested in Lady X weren't they? She drew a long uneven breath, sat down and smiled less frostily as he deftly laced her skating shoes. Probably he had had lots of experience as a lady's man. His bare blond head bent low over his task and she had an idiotic impulse to smooth back the slightly her lap. What a thing to have happen! Determinedly she put it out of her mind. "This air should be good for foggy rumpled waves. Horrors! She clenched her hands tightly in brains, if any," she laughed, in his own vein.

"Pardon? Oh—yes—yes—sure." Cy seemed preoccupied all at once. He tied her laces and quickly changed his own shoes.

The lake was nearly deserted this early in the afternoon and Ellen sighed with pleasure as they swung along over the shining surface. She hoped and prayed they wouldn't encounter a soul they knew or who knew them. She didn't feel like talking today nor like doing any explaining tomorrow. Queer, how Ann had upset her!

"There's something I want to ask you, Nightingale," Doctor Dent said when they reached comparative seclusion at the head of the little lake. "Something I want to talk over with you—er—get your opinion—"

Ellen's heart turned over. Was it true what Ann had said?

"Er—by the way—er—what was Mac hobnobbing with you about right after I left last night? D-did he say anything about me—us?"

Ellen's lip curled in disdain. So that was it? He feared a reprimand from the Chief of Staff. "What do you mean? About our—your—your persistent annoying—pestering—er—intruding—er—" she floundered. "Oh, he's far too big to notice anything so entirely insignificant, and I'm sure you've been very careful not to get caught." She spoke coldly. "Please don't let's talk. I'm tired and I came out here to relax."

"All right, go ahead and relax. No one's stopping you, but just the same, I'm going to tell you my news and you've got to listen, for this is one time when a rendezvous of ours won't be interrupted, I'll guarantee that if I have to brain anyone who butts in. And it is a rendezvous, my dear Nightingale, whether you call it that or not. I've been willing you to come out here since last night—freeze that off if you can. You're here, aren't you?"

Ellen tried to draw her hands away but could not without exerting force and that she disdained to do. She bit her lip, drew a deep breath and forced her nerves to steadiness. He shouldn't upset her!

"All right—go on—tell your big news if you must have an audience."

"Do you know, I adore your enthusiasm, Gaylord. It's so refreshing," he chuckled mockingly.

Ellen refused to answer.

"I've had two jobs offered me, Nightingale, believe it or not. I bet you had no idea I was in such demand, now did you?"

Ellen still said nothing. Two? She had already heard of one.

"One is with Doctor Blakley, the noted psychiatrist, you know—in Boston. Of course you've heard of him—who hasn't? Swell offices, wealthy clients and the prospect of taking over within ten years. How's that for an offer?"

Ellen laughed scornfully. "Why doctor, how thrilling! It was made for you. Aren't you the fortunate one! And when do you take this deluxe practice—er—position?"

"It was offered me last summer when I finished at Bellevue; but I wanted six months or more under MacGowan before I decided on anything definite."

"I don't imagine Doctor MacGowan's example has been much help to you—he's not your type—"

"You'd be surprised," Cy retorted. "The other," he went on unperturbed, "is of course not to be considered for a moment. You see, Doc Howard, out home, wrote offering me his practice. He's getting old and lame and wants to retire. That's a laugh. Does a general practitioner ever retire?" he laughed gleefully as if the picture he conjured was vastly amusing. "Good joke, eh, Nightingale? Imagine the old family doctor refusing to drive twenty miles just because Johnny Jones gets the stomachache from eating green apples! Ha ha! Why don't you laugh, woman?"

"It isn't in the least funny, Doctor Dent."

"My word, gal, you are low!" He shook his head, then went on. "Imagine me as a general practitioner, Nightingale! Doc's been chief medico out there for forty years. Oh, he's made a living—possibly a bit over; said surplus being used to finance a few of the town's derelicts from time to time—what a life!" Again he laughed derisively, throwing back his handsome head in a way Ellen always found exasperating. "Not for me. Mac thinks the Boston job worth considering. I might do worse and then again I might do better. What do you think about it, Nightingale?"

They had stopped beside a group of low-hanging willows and Ellen raised bright, unfriendly eyes to his.

"Grand, Doctor! When do you leave?"

Dent chuckled again and Ellen longed to slap him.

"Oh, not until spring—May, perhaps, or June. So you like the idea of Boston? I was sure you would. How our ideas coincide! We're the same type, remember—under the skin."

"We are not," Ellen denied, hotly.

"Oh, yes we are, Nightingale. Didn't you just urge me to take the Boston job? You believe in taking life by the smooth handle whenever possible just as most of us do, don't you? 'Soft jobs and easy money' should be carved on the escutcheon of all us moderns. All this talk about life of sacrifice is just a pose—don't I know it? Oh, you need not glare at me like that, darling. I know you think you're sincere but you can't fool me. You're an open book to Cyrus Dent, M.D."

"You're impossible!" Ellen whispered stormily. "I'm not looking for an easy job and I despise anyone in our profession who is. It would be just like you to take the Boston job—go and take it! Marry a rich girl who can give you prestige, and live the life of Riley, and see if I care. You'd never do anything as a general practitioner. That job calls for a real man—a big man. A man willing to forget all about ease, money and fame if he can bring healing to the sick and comfort to the suffering. You couldn't do that, Cyrus Dent—you're too light—too fickle—too—too—mercenary. Anyway, you'd be a failure if there was real work to be done and you know it. Play boy!"

"Whew!" gasped the young man. "How you do go on! I always said you were too emotional—too temperamental to spend your life among the sick, and Time—good old Time—has proven me indubitably correct. Okay. Listen to this, Nightingale. Know the reason why I can't take that job out in the sticks? Go into general practice? Don't answer, please. I know what you think or intend to say, which isn't always the same thing, I've noticed. I can't go because you see I should need a helpmeet, as the Scriptures say. One who is willing to go into exile with me and to," he grinned wickedly again as he stared down at her, "protect me from my female patients. An understanding girl—possibly even a trained nurse or at least one who wouldn't fly off the handle if I stayed out all night with a sick—man." He emphasized the noun.

The breath seemed snatched from Ellen's lungs. She felt completely deflated and slightly dashed.

"Oh, my intentions would be quite honorable, I assure you, my good woman. I'd expect to marry her. She might do worse at that, or couldn't she? Of course it all depends on one's point of view. And of course this is all hypothetical. If I go to Boston it won't be so necessary. In fact, I might even be more popular among the dear things if I remained single. Ah me—it's a pity you dislike me; but—do you? I somehow think you don't, and I think you're—

69

well—a nice girl, in spite of your disposition which is sort of tacky to say the least. But I'm sure that could be remedied. Well, what do you think of the idea, Nightingale?"

Ellen found to her annoyance that she was trembling. "I—I—I think you—you're—" she began when she could control her voice.

"Now don't say you don't approve of that either!" he said quickly. "Think about it, lady. It's not such a bad idea. Perhaps, given a chance, I could sell it to you properly."

Ellen stamped her foot angrily which was unfortunate, for she slipped and would have gone down ignominiously if he hadn't caught her—caught her and held her close for a long minute before she tore herself away.

"I'm not getting out for three—possibly four months," he went on, slightly breathless. "Anything can happen in four months. However, Nightingale, I'm glad I told you—that we have had this talk in spite of your exuberant enthusiasm—your joyous hilarity, and I'm sure that from now on you'll not be quite so cold and aloof—so exaggeratedly indifferent." He laughed softly for a moment, then quickly stooped and kissed her squarely on the mouth.

"O-oh—oh!" Ellen cried, unable to decide whether she was more angry than astonished or more astonished than thrilled. What was the matter with her, anway? It wasn't her first kiss by any means; but never before had she been so upset. Hypothetical, was it? The talk of marriage may have been but the kiss was not—that, she knew. Hypothetical, indeed! How silly she was! That job of general practitioner was phony—his idea of a joke. If he had been hinting that she might consider the job of "helpmeet" as he called it, he could get the idea right out of his system. Her pulses steadied. She should give up her precious dream to act as a prop for Cy Dent to lean on! Not in a million years! Braddock had hinted at a possible affair with one of the Country Club crowd. That was his dish. Let him marry money and then he could buy all the help he needed and patronage, too Boston? Of course he would take that job. He intended to all the time. She bit her burning lips. Darn him!

"Just a formality, Nightingale," Cy said softly. "When a man gets sentimental, he always kisses the nearest girl, you know. I'm sure she would feel defrauded if he didn't."

Again Ellen noticeably said nothing. "Sentimental!" she scoffed at herself. "Ye gods! If you've been sentimental, Cy Dent, give me MacGowan's lecture on fractures!"

As if he read her thoughts, Cy took her hands. "Whatever you're thinking at the present moment, Nightingale," he chided, "you're quite unfair—in fact, you're dead wrong. Come on, let's skate."

Two hours later they parted at the corner, a block from the Nurses' Home, without again referring to the subject.

"I suppose he thinks he has only to lift a beckoning finger and every nurse in Anthony Ware will follow. Well, I made it pretty plain to him that I didn't for one moment take his ravings seriously. Or did I?"

As she took off her heavy clothes, Ellen experienced a feeling of dissatisfaction. Cyrus Dent was everything a girl could possibly want and yet he left her cold. Why was that? Was she, as Ann had intimated on occasion, one of those girls entirely lacking the power to love completely? She had heard of such people and had instinctively shrunk from them as monstrosities. She had read somewhere that only a person who had been touched by a great love or a great sorrow—preferably both—was capable of living a great life —doing a great work. But surely there were exceptions— exceptions that proved the rule. Maybe she, herself, was one of those exceptions. The thought wasn't exactly comforting.

She told herself that she was fortunate to have escaped falling in love with Cy. All the other girls adored him. No doubt that was the reason for his persistent attention to her —the unattainable. A sudden smile curved her lips for a moment.

"Here is one nurse, my glamorous Doctor Cyrus Dent, whose sleep you will never disturb. You may be a heartthrob and high blood pressure to the rest of the female population of the globe, but to me you're just a pain in the neck!"

She determinedly closed her mind to the whole affair, changed to her uniform and went down to dinner. Ann grinned wisely at her from across the table. Ellen frowned and bit her lip as she felt herself blushing. The girl was positively uncanny.

CHAPTER NINE

FOR SOME REASON, Ellen and Doctor Dent did not meet again for two days. Ellen cringed in every nerve each time the elevator door opened. How should she meet him? He was quite impervious to snubs and she was in no mood for banter.

Ann was having trouble with a wisdom tooth and was temporarily off duty. Janet Hoyt, a junior student, was subbing for her. Janet was one of those big, placid girls with not a nerve in her body—the kind who make grand matrons of orphanages and asylums. She looked up from the text book she was studying and eyed Ellen with adoring but slightly worried gaze.

"You're—you're terribly jumpy tonight, Miss Gaylord," she stammered. "Don't you feel well? You've been on nights awfully long."

"I'm all right." Ellen was surprised and annoyed to find that she spoke sharply. "I am sort of jumpy, as you call it. I don't know why unless it's the storm. Just listen to that wind."

"Don't you like the wind?" the other girl asked in surprise. "I just love it! I adore being out in a regular gale, especially if there is rain or snow along with it. I love to feel it on my face and to fight it every step of the way—to master it."

Ellen smiled at her. Once, ages ago, that was the way she had felt. When she was at home, she had gloried in the storm's buffeting. Why had she changed? Or had she really changed?

"I like to be out in the wind," she said, "but somehow, when I'm inside it sort of makes me homesick."

"Probably that's it," the other answered.

Ellen went over to the great window at the end of the corridor and drew back the linen curtains. Clouds scudded across the moon leaving long tatters through which an occasional star twinkled faintly. The bare giant elms sighed and bent and writhed as if in agony. It was all eerie and somehow sinister. Ellen shivered and as she drew back, her glance focused on a darker shadow in the shrubbery near the garage. As if aware of her gaze, it shrank and melted into the background. Ellen pulled the curtains together.

How silly and imaginative she was! The night watchman, of course. Since that advertisement he had been particularly alert.

"It's a wild night," she said as she sat down at the table and picked up her own book. "Everyone is restless—there —I knew it," as two summoning red lights glowed. "I'll go. You get on with that chapter."

She supplied the necessary demands of two of L's patients, gave an inquiring glance at little Angela Dubail who appeared frailer and more ethereal each time she looked at her, passed on down the ward to the bed of Lady X and paused for a moment. The girl lay in that same deathlike sleep to which she seemed to fall from time to time. Ellen gently touched her forehead. Cool and slightly moist. Her breathing was so light as to be almost imperceptible. If she were indeed dead, she would look just so, Ellen knew. A feeling of futility overcame her for a moment. In this girl was her own strong, healthy blood—poured into her veins gladly and hopefully. A little flood of warmth crept to her face as she realized that her own blood had been supplemented by Doctor Dent's. She wondered whimsically if the two bloods mixed well or if they, too, quarreled. It was rather odd that they typed alike—odd and vaguely disturbing when Ellen realized how much she disliked the man.

She went back to the corridor. No doubt Cyrus Dent had been indulging in his perverted idea of humor when he spouted his hypothetical cases for her benefit. She was glad she had given him no satisfaction. She bit her lip and suddenly felt uncomfortably warm. She wished—how she wished he hadn't kissed her! She had read somewhere that with every kiss goes a part of one. How silly? Why, or why couldn't she put him out of her mind? "Out damned spot!" she mentally ordered, and giggled aloud just as Doctor Dent arrived from Pediatrics up front at the same time Marcella left the elevator with the midnight sandwiches and coffee.

"Anything new?" he asked impersonally as he perched himself on one corner of the table.

"Not a thing." Ellen was proud of her cool, level voice.

"Mac's expecting Lady X to come out of her amnesia any time now. She's definitely better. See any signs, Gaylord?"

"None at all. I was just looking at her and she appears about as she has for days. To be sure she isn't quite so waxen and she doesn't seem so scared, but otherwise she is just the same."

Dent reached for a sandwich.

"Yours is downstairs, Doctor," Marcella said shortly. "I can't see why you want to eat other people's lunches."

"Can't you, Harris? Well, I'll tell you. Ever hear of Omar Khayyám? 'A loaf of bread, a jug of wine and thou beside me in the wilderness,' etc., etc. Now, if you could find it in your hard and unfriendly heart to stay and share my meal, lady, it might prove more palatable."

"The voice is the voice of Doctor Dent, the interne; but the tone and theme are those of Cyrus Dent, eligible bachelor and idol of the Country Club crowd," Marcella said with her usual bluntness.

"You do me wrong, Lady." Ellen saw that he flushed with annoyance. "In this profession you know it behooves one to be on friendly terms with the townspeople. It's good policy and besides, I need the exercise."

"Umph!" snorted Marcella, and wondered if Ellen had heard that he had been offered a ritzy job in Boston, catering to the neurotic elite.

"Umph me no umphs, Marcella Harris," the young man went on, his natural nonchalance restored. "There isn't a girl in that whole crowd to compare with one we have here in Anthony Ware." He glanced quickly at Ellen and grinned at her quick hot blush. She glared wildly at him and he went on smoothly, an impish quirk on his handsome mouth: "Don't you people think Lady X about the loveliest thing you've ever seen? I'm telling you—that girl is class."

Later when she thought of it, Ellen could not describe her reactions to that statement. She was suddenly sick. She felt the blood drain from her face, and pinched herself to restore her senses. She could not lift her shamed and angry eyes, but swallowed the food in her mouth with the help of coffee which fortunately had cooled considerably. She was sure she knew why people felt a sudden urge to commit murder. The smooth, mocking voice went on:

"We're hoping for a break soon. Do any of you girls want to make a bet with me?"

"What odds?" Marcella asked, not that she wanted to know particularly; but he was eating far too many sandwiches—the pig! and she thought to divert his attention. If only he wasn't so darn good looking and so sort of appealing! It made her mad.

"A nickel to a dime that Lady X is somebody important. Oh-oh—time for gambling internes to scram. 'Bye—Nightingale-s." The 's' was pronounced and he departed as the elevator discharged its passenger—the night watchman.

Marcella giggled maliciously. "That's one time the handsome Dent got fooled," but Ellen had fled to the safety of the ward. There she stayed—smoothing a rumpled coverlet, listening to the irregular breathing of Angela Dubail, murmuring a little prayer in her heart as she looked down at the thin face, the quiet, folded hands entwined with her rosary; adjusting a window.

Her eyes searched the shadows near the garage. It must have been the watchman she told herself again, for now there was no one lurking there.

Just what she feared she couldn't have told. That the wretches who had abused Lady X and left her for dead would never be satisfied to let well enough alone and take their chances at remaining undiscovered, she somehow felt sure. Let Cy Dent laugh at women's intuition if he wanted to, she knew that Doctor MacGowan respected hers. Hadn't he left Lady X right here in L?

A car drove into the courtyard below, its headlights searching out every nook and cranny. No, there was no one down there now. It must have been the watchman. The car lights went out. Ellen turned and went back to her table in the alcove. Marcella had gone and Janet still nibbled at a sandwich. The service elevator whirred up past their floor. Someone was to have an operation—a major one, evidently. She wished she could be up there if MacGowan was operating.

What a waste for Cy Dent to work under Mac! Catering to a lot of silly women nursing imaginary ailments! He made her sick.

The night wore on. At two o'clock the elevator stopped at the fourth floor and a patient was wheeled down the corridor. Ellen went to meet it.

"A new guest for you, Gaylord," Doctor Dent said as he stood aside for the orderly to wheel the stretcher through the door of L. "Emergency appendectomy and just in time. Fortunately, nothing happened—scarcely an inch incision. She'll be all right. Out in ten days. Right here, Joe. Okay?" He turned to Ellen and grinned boyishly. "I still get a big kick out of being on my own."

He walked away and Burns, who was on call that week, said when he was out of hearing:

"Mac couldn't beat that job, Gaylord Swift and sure and perfectly calm—that's Dent. Too bad he'll throw it all away for a passel of white-livered blue-bloods—I mean, his knack of using a knife. Her name is Levin—from down by the tracks somewhere."

Burns departed and Ellen went in to look at Mrs. Levin. So Cy was a good surgeon! She thought he would be from his hands. He had the hands of a surgeon. Boston! He'd get mightly little chance to perform any operations in Boston. He would be working with peoples' minds, if any. He'd be asking about their dreams and digging inquisitively into their past lives. Oh, what a waste! Cy Dent made her absolutely sick!

Fanny Brice drew Ellen aside as she scanned the mystery girl's chart a few minutes after she came on duty the next day. Still no change.

"Our mystery patient has had a caller."

Ellen looked up sharply. "A caller? What sort of a caller?"

"She said she was Nancy Langham—Mrs. Peter Langham from Boston. She insists Lady X is Violet Terrill—her English cousin or second cousin. But although extremely attractive, young, beautiful and smartly gowned, our mystery girl never batted an eye when she saw her. It certainly took the wind out of the lady's sails, but she continued to insist the girl is her cousin. Forsyth was with her and was the old girl oily! What a snob Agatha is!"

Ellen ignored the last. "Is she staying here—in town, I mean? Will she come again?"

"Sure. She's coming tonight. That's why I wanted to see you. Forsyth told her you had sort of taken charge of Lady X and that you might be able to give her some information. I don't know what information you have to give. Lady X is still the same enigma she was when she landed here as far as I can see. I know you and Mac and Dent have been sort of holding prayer meetings over her—"

"Don't be silly. It's an unusual case. Of course we have been, and still are, interested in her," Ellen interrupted.

"Well, so are the rest of us, but not to the same extent. After all, Gaylord, you don't actually know anything about her. She may not turn out to be the angelic visitant you three think she is What was she doing with that gang in the first place? You know molls sometimes come from pretty decent families."

"So I've heard, but Lady X is no moll, Brice," Ellen assured her.

"No? Well, here's wishing you luck!"

Ellen went to the end of the long ward where Lady X lay staring at the ceiling, a frown of perplexity and concentration making her brows a straight, dark line above her big violet eyes.

"So you had a visitor?" Ellen smiled down at the sober face on the pillow.

"Yes." Only that.

"And she didn't mean anything to you? You don't remember ever seeing her before?"

"No."

"Well," Ellen tried to make her voice reassuring, "don't worry about it. It will all come back—soon."

"Oh, I hope so!" It was a wail of despair.

A tall slender young woman on her middle twenties, paused just inside the door. Doctor Dent was with her, his manner admiring and solicitous. Ellen went to them.

"This is Nurse Gaylord, Mrs. Langham," he said, professional suavity so thick it nauseated Ellen. "Miss Gaylord has been much interested in your cousin and perhaps better than anyone here, is able to give you particulars regarding her." He left them and walked over to the mystery patient's bed. Ellen saw the girl's eyes brighten at his approach and noted the smile with which she greeted him.

"You are sure she is your cousin, Mrs. Langham?" Ellen asked. She had been right, Lady X was someone of importance. Mrs. Langham exuded wealth and social position from every pore.

"Oh, absolutely sure. I haven't seen her in six years—not since I visited her grandfather on my honeymoon. To be sure, she was only a child of fifteen or so, but she hasn't changed a great deal except that she is painfully thin. I think she is even prettier, if anything." Mrs. Langham's eyes, violet, too, clouded with pity.

"How did you know about—where she was?" Ellen wanted to know.

"It was the strangest thing! You see, she wrote me when he grandfather died—oh, two months ago, I think it was. It seems she had been quite ill and was only just convalescing. I wrote immediately urging her to come to me for a long visit and she accepted and set December first as the date of her sailing. My brother and she were—shall we say, tentatively engaged for a year or more—at least there had been a sort of understanding between them and something happened last spring—I don't know what, but it was suddenly all off and instead of going to England as planned, he went to South America. But about Vi—on shipboard, she met a girl she had known in boarding school in France—Vivian Townsend—yes, my dear," at Ellen's look of familiarity with the name, "the Vivian Townsend, and they renewed their friendship. Vivian urged Vi to spend the holidays, or at least sometime with her in New York before coming on to Boston. Vi wired me to that effect, saying she was not sure when she would arrive in Boston but was sending on part of her luggage. I was relieved, because the twins came down with measles the next day.

"After that, I heard nothing from her. I was a bit surprised to hear nothing at Christmas time but the boys were pretty sick and I was busy as you can well imagine. And Vi, while a sweet youngster, was never particularly thoughtful of others—spoiled, you know.

"Well, yesterday morning I was having my hair done —the radio was going and I heard a news commentator tell about Lady X. The description fitted Vi and although I had no reason to think it might be she, I felt suddenly terrified and called my husband. Of course he scoffed at my fears, but offered to telephone the Townsend town house in New York. The butler told him the family had gone to Florida. That Miss Terrill, who had spent only a day or two there, had left for Boston on the morning after the Townsends' departure for the South.

"That was three weeks ago! Of course Pete was frantic and I packed a bag and caught the first plane for Brentwood and here I am—and—" the bright face clouded and her eyes filled with tears— "she doesn't know me from Adam. But where was Kent, her maid, all this time? I can't understand how it happened that she was alone. Kent had been her nurse and went everywhere with her. Isn't it strange she doesn't know me? I—"

"She doesn't know anyone—not even herself," Ellen comforted. "But she will — I'm sure of it. I imagine she has had a terrible experience."

Mrs. Langham's hands clenched and her voice hardened. "Hanging is too good for those beasts!"

Doctor Dent joined them. Ellen's lip curled as she noticed how polished his manner had become. "You have no idea how relieved I — we are to find her people, Mrs. Langham," he murmured. He turned to Ellen, very much the doctor and wholly impersonal. "You see, nurse, that publicity did the trick after —"

A piercing scream sent the three scurrying into the ward just as a shot rang out in the courtyard below and echoed through the long room.

CHAPTER TEN

AT THE OTHER end of the ward, Janet Hoyt bent over little Angela Dubail as if to shield her from whatever harm impended. Ellen, seeming to know instinctively it was something pertaining to Lady X, rushed to her bedside, to find she had fainted. The window nearby was partly open and after a moment, Doctor Dent thrust out his head. A small crowd was gathered in the courtyard below, and a dark object lay huddled halfway down the fire escape. Ward L was palpitant with excitement.

"I seen 'im, Doctor. I seen 'im," cried Mrs. Levin, two beds down the ward. " 'E 'issed somethin', and then th' pore thing screamed bloody murder an'—, then'e wasn't there any more."

"Who wasn't there? I'm afraid you're imagining things, Mrs. Levin." Doctor Dent, his face stern, shook his head at the garrulous old woman.

"Imaginin' things, is it?" Mrs. Levin sniffed in offended dignity. "Then what made 'er scream? Tell me that."

But no one answered and, bleak-eyed, she lay and muttered to herself.

The screens, withdrawn during the past few days, were again in place around the mystery girl's bed. Doctor MacGowan, being particularly interested, was summoned but was unavailable and Doctor Braddock came in his stead. The faint was a prolonged one. Mrs. Langham was frightened. There was something sinister in the whole affair.

"Sometimes a shock of this kind proves a blessing in disguise, Madam," Doctor Braddock reassured her "I have known cases where a sudden shock such as this has not only restored the memory but has been instrumental in reviving a dormant nervous system."

Ellen, busy chafing the patient's wrists, heard the House Physician tell the others that the man on the fire escape had been shot by the watchman when he refused to come down. He was badly hurt and was in Emergency right now with MacGowan and Fielding probing for the bullet which had lodged in his groin. Police had been notified.

So she had been right, after all, Ellen told herself, but with no feeling of triumph. While the publicity had undoubtedly found Lady X's friends, it had been the means of arousing her enemies to further deviltry. Yet, why should anyone want to harm this lovely girl?

Came a long, quivering sigh. The violet eyes opened, a look of bewilderment in their purple depths.

"O — oh!" she breathed. "Am I ill?" Her hand, still and lifeless so long, brushed the bright hair from her face She frowned as her eyes met those of Nancy Langham. She smiled questioningly. "Why—why, Nancy! How did you get here?"

"There was an accident, Vi, and I came as soon as I heard. Feeling better?" Mrs. Langham's voice was tremulous.

"Yes—but why can't I move? I—"

"You see, Miss—Miss Terrill," Doctor Dent's voice was gentle, his eyes tender, "your back and head were injured and we had to put you in a cast for a little while. But you are a great deal better and will soon be all right again."

Ellen though: "Either Ann is right and he's fallen hard for Lady X or he's going to be a terribly successful doctor with an enviable bedside manner, but— pity the poor patient if she has a susceptible heart and a weakness for glamorous blond men!"

Violet Terrill shuddered and suddenly began to cry weakly. She clung to Cy's hands. "Such terrible dreams!" she sobbed, then smiled through her tears. "I'm just a great baby to let go like this" To Ellen's further disgust, Doctor Dent's face said quite plainly to her: "Maybe, but you're a most adorable one!"

"The big, soft, fickle idiot!" Ellen's heart stormed. "I hate him How I hate men, especially handsome, blond doctors!"

The House Physician held a glass to the patient's lips, his hand beneath her head. "Too much conversation, I'm thinking," he said gruffly. "Our patient needs quiet and sleep. As my young nephew would say: suppose you scram." He spoke to them all, but looked at Cyrus Dent, who colored and removed his hand from where it lay clasped in the thin one of Violet Terrill. The girl smiled into his eyes and he hastily withdrew.

"Not everyone, please, Doctor." The violet eyes shifted to Ellen. "Stay with me, nurse." Her voice had changed somehow — taken on a note of authority, or did Ellen imagine it?

"All right, but you be quiet, remember. No talking," the doctor ordered. "I know what two girls are when they get together with their back hair down." He glanced at Ellen, his eyes keen.

"You need have no fear, Doctor," Lady X said and Ellen was sure now that her voice was changed. "Why, the little snip is actually putting Doctor Braddock in his place!"

The others withdrew. Lady X lay with her eyes closed. Ellen wondered if she was trying to fill in the gaps that still eluded her. Perhaps she was never to remember that brief black chapter in her life. But the mystery girl was a mystery no longer. X equalled Violet Terrill, cousin of the wealthy socialite, Nancy Langham of Boston, and Ellen ruminated, now ripe and eligible for Cyrus Dent. Was that to be the answer?

Boston? Cy would take that swanky job and eventually marry Violet Terrill and Ellen would be free from him forever. And although she felt she had now settled things smoothly and satisfactorily for all concerned, a tear slid down Ellen's cheek and made a round wet spot on her immaculate uniform. She dabbed at her eyes and grinned shamefacedly.

"Idiot!" she chided, wordlessly. "You know you're thoroughly pleased at the happy and romantic solution. Only —only—you're tired. Snap out of it!" She jerked to attention.

What of the man who had been shot? Who was he? She stole a glance at the window that looked onto the fire escape and shuddered. Just what had he planned doing? Was it one of the abductors trying to enter? And for what purpose, if any? She rose and went to the window. The night was very black. Bright rectangles of light from windows were reflected against the concrete and shrubbery. The fire escape, supposed to be a safety measure, could also prove a menace as tonight had shown. Ellen had no doubt in her mind that the man on the fire escape was one of the kidnappers. She reached up and pushed the lock into place, then pulled down the shade. There was a faint but devout: "Thank heaven!" from Mrs. Levin.

Ellen smiled. There were no visitors in L tonight. No doubt the intense cold had something to do with it. Ellen was glad of the quiet. Callers would only prolong the excitement and tend to produce wakefulness. She walked slowly through the ward, straightening a blanket, adjusting a pillow, adding a word of comfort or advice or, perhaps giving a friendly, understanding little pat to a hand outside a coverlet. It was Ellen's endearing way and Ward L loved it.

"Some excitement you had over in L the other night." Ann Murdock, minus the troublesome wisdom tooth, lay on an exercise mat in the gymnasium and contemplated her carefully manicured nails. "And now Lady X is no longer the honored guest of Sweet Charity. Tell me, Ellen, why do these things always happen when I'm out?"

"Don't ask me, Ann. It was exciting all right, but it certainly wasn't pleasant. They think the man will die."

"So what? You don't expect me to weep over that, do you? If I remember rightly, you were for boiling the whole gang in oil not so long ago."

"I know, and they deserve it," Ellen agreed, "but if this man dies they may never find out who the others are."

"Won't the lady in the case open up?"

"The lady? You mean Violet Terrill? That whole episode is gone as far as she is concerned. She remembers nothing after leaving the Townsends' three weeks and more ago. Perhaps it's as well if she never remembers all the horrors of that time." Ellen turned a complete somersault and bounded to her feet, shaking the hair from her face.

"What does she talk about, Ellen?" Ann asked curiously. "Is she as ritzy as Marcia says?"

"Well, she's English—typically so, and she's sweet, Ann. Everyone's crazy over her beauty and jubilant over her recovery."

"Ye-ah. Watch out for these sweety-pie folks, darling. They're poison. I've had experience with 'em." Her voice hardened. "I notice Dent wearing a particularly fatuous grin when I inquired for her a few minutes ago. They do say he haunts her room. What does Angus think about it?"

"Pleased as can be, of course, especially as her back is coming along so nicely. She can use her legs now, you know. Mrs. Langham wants to take her to Boston as soon as she can be moved."

"Good!" Ann said it emphatically. "She's a menace, I tell you. Dent's completely gaga over her."

Ellen turned another somersault before she made any comment. She, too, had seen the eager light in Cyrus Dent's eyes whenever he entered Violet Terrill's room. And, she told herself stubbornly, she was glad of it.

"Why shouldn't he be?" she asked crisply. "She's charming and Dent's a fine man. However, Ann, your imagination is probably running away with you—again."

"Oh, no, my sweet, not again. You could have had Dent any time you liked during the whole of the past year—well, six months anyway; but you're so darned efficient—so unapproachable—so indifferent to male overtures—so bent on becoming a martyr, that no doubt you cooled—I mean, froze—his ardor. But cheer up, darling, there's still Angus. Had any rendezvous lately? I've sort of lost track since I've been down in Hades."

It was quite useless to be annoyed with Ann. She was just naturally meddlesome and curious. Ellen bit her lip, then laughed lightly. "Did you ever try writing novels, Ann? Why don't you? You manage to see romance in the drabbest, most ordinary occurrences, and you know there have been nurses who became famous writers."

"They should. They see life in the raw," Ann conceded. "I could give the reader an ear—I mean an eyeful, all right. If I see the romance in life, Ellen, I see also the rottenness, the filth, the—well, the malignant side of it, too. You're an idealist. You see mainly the perfection to which you hope to lift the physically, mentally and morally sick. My eyes are open to the plain facts—the slime that will cling to them as long as they live—the slough in which they more often than not wallow—by preference. You see, Ellen, I'm a realist, and aside from the kids who are innocent victims of life and perhaps a few—a very few cases due to unavoidable accidents, the great majority of the patients we get are here because of self-indulgence, laziness, or plain filthiness. Not necessarily of the body—I mean of

84

the mind and soul. I'm just about fed up, Ellen. But I could write a book all right; the trouble is, who would publish it? I should be put away as a perverter of morals. I, who am so moral that it positively hurts!" she laughed shrilly. "It's the selfish people, without morals of any kind, who get the breaks in this world, my child," She continued while Ellen dutifully went on with her exercises. "So," she watched the girl before her with smoldering, green-gray eyes, "I'm chucking all troublesome inhibitions —oh, yes, I have them thar pesky deterrents to success and a good time—believe it or not—I inherited 'em from some sanctimonious ancestor—but I'm chucking 'em and I'm playing my cards so that I'm getting a real break. The case I'm taking on tonight should prove the turning point in my life. A break—that's all I ever needed."

"So? What case is that?"

"Bill Munson, the paper man. Oh, you needn't turn up your nose, Miss Gaylord. He's only a means to an end— and what an end! That's what I keep my eye on, my child, the end—not the means, that doesn't count. Well, as I started to say when your snooty look stopped me, Bill's in seventy-four with a broken leg—his own, I assure you. He came day before yesterday. Hess was on one night. She says he's a villain—worse than any spoiled child she ever had. Wants not only a nurse but a messenger as well. I'll tame him! Holmes is down with a sore throat and I'm taking over. Not for nothing have I been cultivating Agatha these past few days." She laughed maliciously. "How the old girl falls for a bit of flattery! I've been laying it on with a trowel."

Ellen refused the bait. She knew Ann was probably exaggerating as she did even the simplest events, yet she had no doubt the girl had wormed her way into the Superindendent's good graces, using any and all means for the purpose, the while keeping her tongue in her pretty cheek. And although she wondered idly what Ann had done to get around Miss Forsyth, she wasn't interested enough to ask. She didn't have to.

"Can you feature me in the role of Cupid, Ellen?" Ann asked mischievously, still flat on the mat. "I'm not so bad at it, either, though this time it cost me three bucks and I'll have you know that three bucks are three bucks in this institution."

Ellen tossed high a medicine ball and caught it without, apparently, having heard. A group of girls left the ping pong tables in favor of the pool. Ann and Ellen had the big gymnasium to themselves.

"Know what I did?" Ann's voice became confidential. "I bought two tickets for last night's Symphony at the High School auditorium — the seats side by side. I mailed one to Angus and the other to Agatha. Compliments of the Orchestra. Agatha's tight as a drum and Angus is Scotch, so of course I was sure they would use them. I owe Angus one for bawling me out last week.

The pill! I know Aggie feels that Angus, while far beneath Braddock, is but little lower than the angels.

Imagine them at the concert and, she closed her eyes and grinned wickedly, "fancy the glorious—hic—surprise when they discovered themselves seatmates! Angus, who hates women and wouldn't be seen in public with one of the creatures! Would that be a swell tale to discuss over the Brentwood teacups! Don't look so darned disapproving, Miss Gaylord—and listen—this will slay you! I went to Agatha's sanctum this morning and just sort of hinted that I'd seen the Chief buying tickets—I didn't say when or where — didn't have to, she fell all right and blushed to her ears. Her eyes got sort of soft and she just looked off into the rose-colored distance and I fancied she was probably hearing bagpipes a-skirling and seeing bony-kneed old Angus in kilts—imagine! I had to know if she went so I asked if she liked Symphonies. She assured me that she had enjoyed last night's concert very much, and listen, she said:

"It was generous and thoughtful of Doctor Mac-Gowan to give Doctor Braddock and me that delightful evening.'"

"Wow! Was I surprised! And what a scandal that's going to make in this burg! Fancy Braddock and Agatha! No one will believe they weren't actually together. And old lady Braddock about ready to pass out! I'd give a good deal to know if Angus smelled something fishy about those tickets or if he's wise to them being sweet on each other and was himself playing Cupid. I'd give a good deal to know."

Ellen still said nothing.

"While she was in that soft mood, I worked on her," Ann went on. "Hoped I'd soon get a chance at a private case again—blah-blah-blah. Then I switched to the subject of her fairness, more blah-blah-blah. Before I left the office she had changed me from nights in the Gossip Shop to nights in seventy-four. That's what I call using the old bean, Ellen. Eh, what?"

"And some bright day you're going to find that 'old bean' of yours landing you in a peck of trouble, Ann Murdock. Honestly, I can't see why you do such crazy things," Ellen cried, exasperated at the other's smug grin.

"Of course you don't, darling Stiff-in-the-morals. You are two-thirds vegetable like all the rest of the bunch in this hospital—this whole town, for that matter. I'd go stark, raving mad if I didn't kick over the traces once in a while." She kicked up her heels, then lay inert once more, watching the other girl with bright, slyly mocking eyes.

"A grand nurse you're going to make," Ellen told her severely, although she didn't swallow half the trash Ann had been handing out.

"Uh-uh." Ann's bright head rolled from side to side in quick denial. "I couldn't live up to that Pledge if I tried, Ellen. Sin entered into me at birth — a double dose of it. That pledge is for you, my sweet," She mocked and began a slow intoning. " 'I solemnly pledge myself before God, and in the presence of this company, to pass my life in purity and to practice my profession faithfully. I will abstain from whatever is deleterious and mischievous'—imagine! Me! 'and will not take or knowingly administer any harmful drug. I will do all in my power to maintain and elevate the standard of my profession'—that's a laugh! — 'and will hold in confidence all personal matters committed to my keeping and all family affairs coming to my knowledge in the practice of my calling. With loyalty will I endeavor to aid the physician in his work' — aid them? We do most of it — all that really counts, anyway—'and devote myself to the welfare of those committed to my care.' Ah-aha-ah-a-aaha-men!" Her unmusical voice rose raucously and Ellen couldn't repress a giggle although she was instantly ashamed. That pledge was sacred to her—something to be carried like a torch, high and white and ever burning. She knew Ann's eyes were on her hoping she would be shocked.

"I'll be out of this dump before June, Ellen." Ann said, defiantly. "I'll not be a nurse much longer, thank heaven!"

"Before June? Now what?" Ellen came and looked down at her with troubled eyes. "Has Tip decided that it's you, after all?"

A shadow flitted across Ann's lovely mobile face for a moment, and was gone. She gave a hard little laugh. "Tip? Who is Tip? Oh, yes, Tip — there was a Tip, wasn't there? No, it's nothing so infantile as Tip Waring nor Cyrus Dent either." She sprang to her feet and slipped her arm through Ellen's. "Come on, Precious, let's do a jump-in-jump-out and then to work!"

Ellen knew the incident was closed and if she wondered just what Ann was planning, she gave no sign. They spent the next few minutes in the pool, then, arm in arm, went down the long corridor and up the stairs to their rooms.

CHAPTER ELEVEN

DOCTOR MACGOWAN came to Violet Terrill's room soon after Ellen went on duty that same evening. Again he was in hospital white. Ellen knew that an emergency operation had been performed on Mrs. Slavonski. She felt a deep pity for the woman and was anxious for news of her.

"Came through splendidly," Doctor MacGowan assured her. "Too bad her gude-for-naught man could not be reached. Now, how is our patient?"

Since the night when he had paid her a call in Ward L, the Chief of Staff had been most affable on those occasions when their paths had crossed and once or twice had singled her out for special attention at clinic and lecture. Aside from the knowing glances with which Ann favored her on those occasions, Ellen saw no significance in the contacts and she was sure neither did anyone else, least of all Miss Forsyth or they most certainly would have ceased.

On this evening, the surgeon examined Miss Terrill, pronounced himself highly satisfied with her progress and then announced that she was to be allowed to leave the hospital next day. An ambulance was arriving from Boston early in the morning, with a doctor and nurse in attendance. Mrs. Langham entered while they were discussing the trip.

"I'm going to miss her," Ellen said warmly. "That's the one drawback to nursing. One does get attached to one's patients. And we have all been so interested in Lady X."

Mrs. Langham smiled. "Vi's a nice youngster—always was. I'm afraid she's been badly spoiled. She can be annoyingly wilful and stubborn at times."

Ellen wondered if she referred to Vi's engagement to her brother.

"By the way, just who is this Dent man? Oh, I know he is interning here; but who is he?"

So Mrs. Langham had noticed his interest in her cousin. Before Ellen could answer, however, Doctor MacGowan drew her aside.

"I'm wondering if you would care to visit a patient of one of my colleagues. A most interesting case; the injury to the spine quite similar to Miss Terrill's. Would tomorrow afternoon be convenient?"

Ellen was startled. What would the Superintendent say? It just wasn't done. Still if the Chief of Staff wanted her to go, why wasn't it all right? After all, it was strictly in the line of duty, wasn't it? Of course. How silly she was! That was due to Ann's nonsense. A little while ago she would have thought nothing of it.

"Thank you, Doctor MacGowan — it is kind of you to suggest it. At what time?"

The surgeon's face was slightly flushed, he fidgeted somewhat and it amused Ellen to know that he was actually nervous at asking her. The great MacGowan! Quite unconsciously he sighed—probably in relief, Ellen felt sure.

"Will three o'clock be too early? Shall you have rested sufficiently?"

"Three will do nicely, Doctor." Ellen smiled up at him, her frank brown eyes friendly.

"Good! May I suggest that you dress warmly? It will be a long drive. Good night—El—er—Gaylord."

"Well!" Ellen murmured to herself as she watched the tall, white-clad, somewhat ungainly figure disappear through the door. "What a break for me that Ann Murdock didn't hear that! And I hope to goodness no one sees me go off with him tomorrow afternoon. If they do, something will happen. Darn that Ann! She's managed to make a self-conscious idiot out of me."

Shots in quick succession — the sound of running feet along the corridor—a policeman's shrill whistle and the long eerie siren of the patrol car, shattered the evening's comparative quiet. Violet Terrill's eyes widened in sudden terror and Ellen quickly shut the door, standing with her back against it as if to keep whatever threatened from entering. She felt a sudden pressure and the handle turned.

"Who is it?" she asked, exerting all her strength to prevent entrance.

"Me—Dent. Are you all right, Ellen? Let me in."

Ellen stood aside. Dent's face was drained of color,

but he managed a wry grin as he caught her hand in a sudden hard grip.

"You win, Nightingale," he murmured. "That publicity stunt wasn't such a hot idea after all."

"O-oh, Doctor!" moaned Violet and Cy turned to the bed.

"Don't be scared," he said soothingly. "Just a wounded bad man we've been harboring for the police. His pals came to get him and fell into a trap. There," as the police siren shrilled again, "there they go, and good riddance to bad rubbish, say we all. Don't tell me a big girl like you is scared! Look at Nightingale there—cool and calm as—as—an iceberg."

Nancy Langham raised an eyebrow, her look quizzical. Ellen forced an aloof smile; her lips felt stiff, and she gave a strangled gasp as Cyrus Dent toppled sidewise and lay huddled on the floor beside the bed. Violet Terrill screamed. Ellen found herself on her knees beside him, his head in her lap. The floor nurse rushed in—Doctor MacGowan, who couldn't have been far off, followed. A stretcher was summoned and Doctor Dent was taken to the operating room, all in the space of a few minutes.

Horrified and confused though she was, Ellen attempted to quiet the terrified Violet who shrank from a spot of blood on the snowy coverlet. Someone swabbed the floor beside the bed and Ellen and the floor nurse deftly changed the stained linen.

"Oh, Nan, take me away!" Violet moaned. "This horrible—this beastly place!"

"All right, dear. We're leaving tomorrow morning quite early," her cousin soothed.

Ellen bit her lip. Not a word about Cy. Oh, suppose he was badly hurt! Mac appeared terribly concerned. She had never seen that look of alarm on his face before. And the way he knelt beside her on the floor and after a quick examination, took Cy's head into his own arms — as if it were something precious — something infinitely dear to him. She looked at the whimpering girl on the bed with something akin to dislike. Selfish! she accused silently; selfish and spoiled!

But the girl was a nervous wreck — she ought not to censure her. Yet, even she, who had actually disliked the man, felt sick and weak at the thought of his possible critical injury. Just what had happened? And where had he been hurt? She wished someone would tell her. Suspense was awful — a terrifying demon that sapped one's strength and undermined one's reason.

Nancy Langham looked up. "I hope Doctor Dent isn't seriously injured. What could have happened?" She spoke in a whisper.

"You asked about him, Mrs. Langham," Ellen said quickly, for some reason feeling called upon to champion him. "Doctor Dent's a grand boy and a fine doctor. I believe he is planning on going in with one of your Boston specialists in the spring. Surely you wouldn't object—if it is serious, I mean?" Now why did she ask that? It was none of her business. She glanced at Violet again. She lay with her hands covering her eyes, little whimpering moans coming from her slightly parted lips.

Nancy Langham smiled. "Object, Miss Gaylord? You mean Vi and he? What good would that do? No, my dear, I have discovered that it is quite useless to interfere in love affairs. I only hope that my brother hasn't been permanently hurt. I don't think I could quite forgive that. He seemed to care a great deal for Vi. You see, she is is really Lady Violet Terrill — she dropped her title during this visit because she wanted complete rest and quiet. She has a large estate in Devon and quite a lot of money, but that would make no difference if Vi loves this good looking young medico and decides to marry him. But—oh, it is all probably just—what do you call it? propinquity. When she leaves, she will no doubt forget—I shall be so glad to get her away!"

Doctor MacGowan hurried down the corridor. Ellen and Mrs. Langham barred the door. "Everything is quite," he said crisply. His eyes searched Ellen's face. "Doctor Dent was shot just below the shoulder—not at all serious. I hope you weren't frightened!"

"Oh, this frightful place!" moaned Violet, hands still over her eyes. "I wish I had never come to the States."

"You'll soon forget all this, darling," Mrs. Langham

assured her. "Wait 'till you see Terry and Petey—they'll change your entire viewpoint. If you're able to travel, we'll go South until spring and then to Cape Cod where the stiff sea breezes will put you on your feet in no time at all." She smiled demurely at the lovely girl on the bed. "If you hadn't come, you would never have met Doctor Dent, darling." She said the last softly—teasingly.

Violet's eyes sparkled and she watched Ellen closely as she said softly: "Isn't he sweet, Nan?" Doctor MacGowan turned his back and walked over to the window. Ellen felt sure he wasn't pleased. His mouth was grim and his eyes that frightening icy gray. "And did you know that he gave me his blood when I first came?"

Ellen had drawn into the background, she didn't want to hear any more. Now, as Doctor MacGowan turned and cleared his throat preparatory to making some remark which Ellen felt sure wouldn't have tended to enhance the patient's self esteem, she laid a small, firm hand on his arm.

"I'm glad it's over," she said quietly. "I haven't felt easy since Lady X came."

"This will give the local constabulary a topic of conversation for a long, long time," the doctor said gruffly and laid his hand over hers for a moment. "Braw laddies, our local police. I doubt if New York's finest could have done better under the circumstances."

"Some time I want to hear the whole story of tonight's fracas," Ellen said.

"Oh, you wull—a thousand times I hae na doot—doubt," he jeered. "That's the worst of small towns, they harp so everlastingly on a single string." He hurried away.

The look in Violet Terrill's eyes puzzled Ellen. She had seen that same look in the eyes of her twelve year old niece when she was preparing to acquire—without leave—her sister's pet blouse or new sweater. She had recognized it when Ann eyed another girl's attractive man and had watched Mrs. Braddock as she was so obviously polite to Miss Forsyth.

Ellen thought Violet Terrill above greedy acquisitiveness. Surely she had never needed to exert herself to win favor with anyone. Beautiful, wealthy, socially secure

—why, men must have literally besieged her with their attentions. Surely she didn't find it necessary to resort to the wiles of a coquette to ensnare Cyrus Dent. An idea thrust through her musings. Did Violet think she was interested in Doctor Dent? She blushed at the thought. Or, did she have the preposterous notion that the handsome Cyrus was interested in her? Her eyes sparkled reminiscently. Absurd! To him, she was just someone on whom he might whet his perverted sense of humor. Knowing she was quite indifferent to him, he delighted in baiting her. That was all. She had no illusions regarding Doctor Cyrus Mansfield Dent. And Violet Terrill could save her ammunition for some more dangerous rival.

Violet and Mrs. Langham were talking in low tones. Suddenly Violet called:

"Nurse Gaylord — please find out if Doctor Dent will be able to come to me before I leave in the morning."

"I doubt it, Miss Terrill," Ellen said, and was unaccountably glad that he wouldn't. "But I will inquire, if you like."

"Of course. Why else should I ask?"

Nancy Langham smiled apologetically. Ellen flushed and left the room. She delivered the message to Thompson, Doctor Dent's nurse, and that young woman made a flat denial — laughing at the absurdity of the request.

"What's the matter with her?" Thompson sputtered irately. "Does she think Doc's putting on an act? Perhaps for her especial benefit? He probably did save her life if she only knew it. Absolutely no. Tell her Doctor Dent won't be out of bed in a week— make it a month —two months." She patted Ellen's arm. "Murdock had her number all right, Gaylord — Lady X is a menace and after all you did for her; but that's life, especially a nurse's life."

Ellen only half heard. Was Cy really badly hurt? There was a little tugging pain at her heart.

"Just what happened, Thompy? she asked.

"We-ll, he happened to be in with forty-three when these two men breezed in. Forty-three was talking sort of crazily and the bigger of the visitors said to Doc: 'We're not satisfied with Joe's progress, see? We're taking him

94

away, now.' Doc faced them and Burns, who happened
in the doorway when they first came, and lingered—
Burns never misses a trick, does she?—said he was cool
as all getout. He said: 'That' what you think; but he's
not going.' The big man snarled: 'We've settled with the
dame and now we'll settle with—' and pulled a gun and
Doc rushed him. Burns screamed—she would—and ran
and she said she never saw anything like the way police-
men poured into that corridor. And when she went back
to forty-three, the patient was dead and Doc had disappeared. Then came the siren scream of Her Royal
Highness and Doc's romantic collapse beside her bed.
That's the story without any trimmings. He's still dopey.
They had to probe for the bullet but he'll be all right.
So, darling, go back and tell her ladyship that there will
be no last minute visit from Romeo tomorrow and if
there are any billets-doux, the hospital minions will take
care of them. Bah! I thought he had more sense!"

Ellen went down the long corridor to Lady Violet's
room. How mistaken she had been in this girl! Dumb,
plain dumb, Ellen Gaylord! Everyone else in the hospital put Lady X down as selfish, supercilious and
greedy, while only she held to the opinion that she was
something precious and altogether lovely. And surely
when she had lain there, lost and frightened, she had
not been like this. Instead, she had clung to Ellen—
been sweetly grateful for her tenderness and care. She
thought back to the moment when she had first noticed
her apparent attraction to Doctor Dent. Why, it was on
the very day the advertisement had first appeared in the
Brentwood Daily Herald. And she had been so thankful
that Lady X was beginning to take an interest in her
surroundings! Well, what about it? Surely she wasn't
jealous! She quickened her step. Cy had always insisted
she was somebody — that she was the prettiest girl he had
ever seen. Hadn't he? Well, why hadn't she been prepared
for this denouement instead of feeling half sick over it?
Surely Doctor Dent was old enough and had had experience enough to pick the wife he wanted, and if he
had decided on Lady Violet Terrill, why, that was his
affair and none of her business in the least.

"Well?"

"Doctor Dent will be confined to bed for some time, Miss Terrill," Ellen said evenly. "He is still unconscious."

Violet covered her eyes again and moaned softly: "Oh, this beastly place — I hate it!"

Mrs. Langham shrugged eloquently. "Buck up, Vi," she urged briskly. "After all, you know, they've been very decent to you here. I doubt if you'd have received better treatment anywhere—even in dear old London," she finished demurely. Then, changing the subject, she said tactfully: "So Kent broke her hip just before you sailed. I'm wondering how you managed without her— you're such a helpless creature."

"Oh, Viv shared her Marie with me coming across and while I was in New York—" her eyes clouded and she frowned in perplexity. "That's odd. I don't recall boarding a plane—"

"Never mind." Mrs. Langham hastened to divert her thoughts. "So Doctor Dent is coming to Boston? She asked the question of Ellen who was busy about the room.

"I understand he has a most attractive offer from one of your specialists."

"Splendid! Then we shall no doubt see something of him. Isn't that fine, Vi?" her cousin enthused.

But Lady Violet Terrill said nothing. She had no doubt reached a blank wall in her memory and was trying to find a way through.

It was two days later that a clear and authentic account of the abduction of Violet Terrill appeared in the Brentwood Daily Herald. The paper took all the credit for discovering Lady Violet's relatives and for the rounding up of the notorious Giotti gang. Out of that incident two men who worked on the Herald received flattering offers from Metropolitan papers. One of them went — the other stayed. He was the editor and couldn't be pried loose from his beloved desk.

The Terrill snatch was just a case of mistaken identity. The Giotti gang was out to get Vivian Townsend and it wasn't until they reached a point west of Albany that they discovered that their victim was not the wealthy Adrien Townsend's beautiful daughter, but a girl of whom they had never even heard, and they lost no time in disposing of her belongings and of her body. They had supposed the tap on the head they had given her when she showed signs of coming out of the chloroform had proven fatal. So they tossed her from their car and sped away, confident of complete safety.

"Well, they will have a long time for reflection," Ellen thought, as she finished reading the lurid account. "It's a blessing it turned out so well and it's to be hoped Lady X never remembers that one dark spot in an otherwise happy visit to America." Ellen felt sure her visit would be happy in spite of her hospitalization. For had not that stay at Anthony Ware brought her love and Cyrus Dent?

CHAPTER TWELVE

ANTHONY WARE slipped quickly back to normal after the arrests of Violet Terrill's abductors. It wasn't even a nine days' topic of conversation among the nurses, for an epidemic of influenza struck Brentwood and the surrounding vicinity and life became far too hectic, and backs and feet too weary for their owners to take an interest in what was now a closed book.

Doctor Dent continued to be a popular and interesting convalescent and his room became a bower of expensive floral offerings and the rendezvous of Brentwood's elite. Members of the staff took to dropping in as they passed his door—only Ellen avoided the vicinity of his room.

Marcella Harris brought her a message from him. Marcella gave it reluctantly. Cy Dent had had far too much fuss made over him as it was. He hadn't done anything especially heroic that she could see. Simply refused to allow an injured man to be removed from the hospital while the policeman on guard had been inveigled into leaving his post for a few minutes. He happened to get in the path of a stray bullet, that was all, and to see and hear the way those silly girls fussed over him was positively sickening. Miss Forsyth, too. The Superintendent intimated that Doctor Dent had prevented them from going to Miss Terrill's room and silencing her forever, but Cy pooh-poohed that story.

Marcella knew that letters and a package of books had arrived from Boston for him and that there had been daily telephone inquiries from the same source. Marcella was inclined to believe it all merely the reaction of a grateful patient. But Ellen knew it for what it was—the interchange of affectionate regard. That Cy had answered these messages she had not the slightest doubt. Of cours he had.

"He said to tell you he had received further details a subject in which you were both interested, Ellen," Marcella told her. "He said to tell you to drop in around six tonight when the mob would have departed."

"Oh, he did, did he? Well," said Ellen, viciously thrusting the needle, with which she had been mending

98

her best pair of stockings, into the pin cushion, "you may may tell him for me that I'm not interested now, never was and never will be. Boston!" she muttered. Then after a moment in which she scrutinized her darning, "Marcella, could you feature our glamorous Cyrus Dent in the role of country doctor, say, or even a small town general practitioner, with unpolished shoes, baggy pants and driving a dusty, disreputable flivver over impossible roads in all kinds of weather—day and night— maybe just to ease an old man's lumbago or bring Mrs. Mooney's unwanted eleventh brat into an uncaring world?" She laughed without mirth. "Well, you never will, for he's going with Doctor Blakley, the swanky psychiatrist—one hundred bucks per office call—more if he goes to the home."

"Say, what's the matter with you, Gaylord?" Marcella asked curiously. "You sound decidedly acid and it's strange for I never knew you to be peevish. I bet it's all that night work. Better get out as soon as you can or they'll commandeer you for private duty. Every bed in the place is filled and not a nurse available. For heaven's sake, Ellen, don't you get sick."

"No," Ellen said, moresely, "I won't get sick. I never get sick."

There was a knock on the door and at her sharp, "Come!" a round-eyed probie entered.

"I can see it's bad news," Ellen said gloomily. "Spill it!"

"Miss Forsyth says for you to report for duty at seven tonight in room thirty-four. Irene Ball is down with laryngitis." Her eyes grew rounder and her voice full of awe tinged with envy. "I passed Murdock on the stairs and she told me that Robert Cooper is in thirty-four staging a comeback. What did she mean? And is it really him? And did you know he has been here before? Miss Ball never told it—the selfish old meanie!"

Ellen frowned. Ann was given to cryptic remarks but this was one she didn't quite get. Marcella laughed. "Remember just before Christmas a man was brought in with a bad knee and Ann insisted it was Robert Cooper? But that man lived in Boston, didn't he?"

"I don't know. I don't remember much about it," Ellen said. "So I'm in for private duty for a while am I? Oh, I don't care what I do, but I hoped I could have my four days next week. Probably that's out, now."

"Sure, it's out. MacGowan's working night and day and even Agatha is helping out. The four oxygen tents are in use and we've sent to New York for two more. Corinth offered one but Mac wanted two. I went out to dinner last night and inadvertently sneezed—wow! Now I know how an untouchable feels. It wasn't anything—just dusting off my brain—if any. But the town is scared stiff. Only the Country Club crowd seems unawed by the epidemic— they continue to troop into Dent's room in one unbroken stream. Just what is this thing you are both so vitally interested in, Ellen?" she asked as the door closed after the messenger.

"Who said it was vital, Marcy?" Ellen demanded.

"We-ll, maybe nobody actually said so, but Doctor Dent seemed pretty excited about it. He sat propped up in bed looking like a slightly inebriated god, his hair tousled, his cheeks flushed and a gleam in his eye that bodes no good to whoever attempts to thwart him. I think I should see what he wants, if I were you, Ellen. Have you been in at all since he's been laid up?"

"Why should I?" Ellen asked defiantly.

"Well, and why shouldn't you? Everyone else has."

"All the more reason why I shouldn't, then," Ellen snapped.

Marcella stared for a moment in mild surprise. What ailed her? Surely she hadn't taken the young man seriously. No one in her right mind would do that. Cyrus Dent was just an irrepressible boy—he ragged them all.

"No," Ellen went on more calmly. "Doctor Dent can get along very nicely without this particular caller. He can have nothing important to say to me and I'm sure I shouldn't be able to be as entertaining and amusing or even as adoring as his visitors. Anyway, I'm busy and can't spare the time."

"Okay," Marcella said and nothing more. Soon afterward, she left.

Ellen found the patient in thirty-four white and big-eyed. He was cross and apologetic by turns. But Ellen knew he had been desperately ill. He did look like Robert Cooper, only she thought him better looking in spite of his need of a haircut and a shave. His name, she found, was Terrill Morley; his occupation, consulting engineer; his home, Boston. Terrill; she wondered if it were a family name and if he were related to Violet Terrill, but of course that wasn't at all likely. Mrs. Langham had spoken of her brother, Terry; but there must be hundeds of Terrys in the world. And yet there was a look of Mrs. Langham in his face—his eyes, which, like hers, were deep violet. He dozed restlessly the forepart of the night, rousing to mutter imprecations on his weakness.

It was nearly two o'clock when Ellen heard a faint sound outside the door. The floor nurse, probably. She put down her book and listened. There it was again. The door opened suddenly and someone slipped in. Doctor Dent, a dressing gown partly covering his pajamas, his left arm in a sling. Ellen got quickly to her feet.

"What are you doing here?" she demanded, her heart almost suffocating her with its hammering.

"How's the patient?" Doctor Dent asked impersonally. "I had to know—I—I was worried." He grinned down at her.

"O-oh! Do you know him?" Ellen asked, feeling herself a fool for imagining he had come to see her.

"Know him? Not from Adam," he answered, brazenly. "But I felt like a rendezvous with you and so—here I am. Remember, Nightingale, I'm a sick man—a patient in this hospital of which you are a staff member. Also, that it is never wise to cross or distress a patient, so you'd better submit gracefully. You stubbornly refused to come when I sent for you, so I have risked pneumonia and perhaps worse to come to you. I hope you appreciate it but of course you don't. Ungrateful wench!"

"Just what did you want to see me about, Doctor Dent?" Ellen managed, though her legs threatened to let her down.

"We really can't talk properly here, Nightingale," he said coolly. "If I go now and so relieve you of the fear of discovery, will you come to see me tomorrow—today—this afternoon?"

"Discovery? I don't know what you mean, Doctor Dent," Ellen flared.

"Well, you're entertaining a member of the staff while on duty, aren't you? I'll grant you it's not especially cordial entertainment, but nonetheless it's entertainment of a sort, and so is a major offence—if found out. Oh, come now, darling, I'm only teasing. Don't be so stiff. Can't you appreciate a bit of pleasantry?" For Ellen had stalked to the door and flung it wide. She could not speak.

"Get out, you!" came unexpectedly from the bed. "Can't you see the lady doesn't like your company? Beat it, fellow or I'll smack you down!"

The intruder ignored the peremptory order.

"You'll come?" he urged, his foot preventing the door from closing.

Where was Hess who was supposed to be on floor duty tonight? Cyrus Dent, with uncanny malice, read her queseting glance.

"Oh, Hess knows her place, dear Nightingale. She's down in forty-two, telling a bedtime story to old lady Talbut."

"At two in the morning?" jeered Ellen, relieved that no one had witnessed this latest bit of effrontery.

"Talbut respects neither time nor place, darling—I will too call you darling if I like, and if you're not careful I'll add a possessive pronoun to it—in public."

"Will you go?" she hissed. "You are disturbing my patient."

"Are you still there?" came from the bed.

"I'll go if you promise to see me this afternoon. Promise?"

"All right," she agreed grudgingly. "Only go— please!"

"I'm practically gone, my darling Nightingale," he whispered, and slipped silently down the corridor to the stairs.

Ellen went back to her patient. He lay with his knees making a small mountain of the blankets, a knowing smile on his lips, his eyes unnaturally bright.

"A persistent chap, eh what?" he said, conversationally.

"Persistently annoying," Ellen agreed. "Most unethical, if you ask me."

"Did I?" He studied her for a moment through narrowed lids. "Say, did anyone ever tell you how perfectly corking you are? Beautiful as a dream, especially when you're mad. I can't say that I altogether blame Pajamas for his persistence. What's he doing here, anyway?"

"He's a member of the staff," Ellen told him. "Now, please be quiet and don't talk any more. You need sleep. Are you quite comfortable? Here." She thrust a thermometer into his mouth and he winkled his nose at her. No, his fever hadn't risen, in fact he seemed better. She shook down the mercury and wiped the instrument.

"Let's talk," the young man said, settling himself more comfortably in bed. "What's your name?"

"No." Ellen was stern. "You've simply got to be quiet. If you talk your temperature will rise again and you'll be worse. Just relax and try to sleep."

He lay quiet for a moment, then:

"Was that Dent? Doctor Dent who just sneaked in here?"

"Why—why, yes," Ellen stammered. "Do you know him?"

"No, I don't; but I intend knowing him. Sis wrote me some nonsense about his saving Vi Terrill's life." His eyes brooded and he scowled.

"Then you are Mrs. Langham's brother, Terry?" Ellen said. "I've been wondering. You look a little like her—but I thought she said you went to South America after Vi—"

"Jilted me!" he growled—"Say it. I don't mind—now. That's what she did. And know why? Because I refused to live in 'Deah ol' Devon' and become a country squire. And me an engineer! I loved the girl, too—crazy about her yet, worse luck! So that's the wonderful Dent? Where are his eyes that he's left you in circulation, beautiful? D'you know, I think I sort of like this place. I didn't at first."

"Suppose you listen and I'll ask the questions?" suggested Ellen, noting his determination to talk. "How does it happen that you're in Brentwood again? You were here just before Christmas, weren't you? With an injury to your leg or something of the sort?"

Young Morley's eyes stared. "Uncanny! Say, I'm highly flattered that you remember me. But where were you? I'm sure you weren't in evidence or I'd certainly have remembered."

"No." Ellen laughed. "One of the nurses declared that Robert Cooper was in Receiving—"

"Robert—! Heck, woman, what did I ever do to deserve that dirty crack? I'm no matinee idol—"

"Well you do look a little like him," Ellen insisted. "But you haven't answered my question."

"The first time, I came to consult Hinman about that Walton Dam project—I've been over at the dam for ten days now—or it was ten days ago I landed in Walton. Where've you kept yourself the week I've been here?"

"Up in L—the free ward."

He laughed weakly. "Don't say that fast, lady, or you might by chance speak the truth. I know what those charity wards are."

"Not from experience, I'm sure," Ellen began indignantly.

"No; but by keen observation."

"You haven't seen our free ward, then. Anthony Ware is proud of its free ward," she spoke stiffly. The condescension of the very rich!

"If you are up there I can well believe it. But tell me about this sudden crush of Vi's. Sis wrote me she had been in an accident—she didn't say what, and had been brought here. She wrote that a Doctor Dent had been very kind to her—had indeed saved her life and that in consequence, Vi had fallen hard for him. Is he such a wiz, that he could save her life, and how?"

Ellen wondered why Mrs. Langham hadn't written the whole truth about the affair and why Terry Morley hadn't read about it all in the papers. But she didn't profess to know the peculiar methods of the rich and to what extremes they would go to avoid or kill notoriety or undue publicity. Well, it wasn't up to her to explain, so she merely said:

"Oh, Doctor Dent gave her a blood transfusion —"

"Whose blood?"

"Why, his own, to be sure. Doctor MacGowan did the actual transfusing."

"I don't think I like that. Why was his blood used? Surely—"

"Oh, don't be alarmed," Ellen told him shortly. "I gave some of mine, too. Speed was needed—there was no time to lose and Doctor Dent and I were both on duty and fortunately typed the same as she. It happens now and then you know, and it's not always possible to find people in the same social set who are willing to give their—"

"Oh, shut up!" the young man said crossly. "You make me sick."

Ellen stared in amazement. Who did he think he was that he could tell her to shut up?

"You know darned well I didn't mean that. No doubt your blood's quite as good or even better than Vi's. She's romantic, you see, and it put her under obligation to him."

"I don't know about that," Ellen contradicted. "She felt not the slightest obligation to me, I assure you."

Terry Morley laughed again, his eyes knowing. "I do believe you're sore at Vi. Well, you're not the first gal she's —well—overlooked. Vi isn't so popular with her own sex, but lord! how the boys fall for her! She's going down to the shore with the family some time next month, Sis wrote, and has expressed a desire to see me again. I have a notion I'll not be going. Walton's only six miles from Anthony Ware and things are sort of looking up with me. I'll see Dent and pass the invitation on to him."

"No doubt the change will be good for him," Ellen agreed, and insisted to herself that she hoped he would go.

There was quiet for a few minutes while the young man seemed to ponder many things. At last he turned his head and stared into her eyes raised questioningly to his.

"Why was Dent pestering you?"

Ellen was startled. She must be careful. "Pestering me? Doctor Dent wouldn't pester anyone. Why, he's—he's a member of the staff."

"So you said; and you also said he was annoyingly persistent. What about?"

"Oh—he wanted my advice about something or other and I haven't had time to take it up with him." She decided to put on a good act. "The doctors in this place think we nurses have nothing to do but wait on them. Let him settle his own problems—I have mine and I don't see anyone giving me any help."

The young man eyed her for a moment before he said whimsically. "So you and Dent typed the same as Vi and blood from you both is at this moment chasing merrily about in her aristocratic veins. What are you carrying the hatchet for? I think the bloke sort of fancies you, lady. Ever consider that angle? Well, don't, for I'm going to give him and all others, active competition from this time forward. Understand?"

"Don't be silly," Ellen said sharply. "And now, for heaven's sake turn over and go to sleep. It's four o'clock and soon your breakfast will be coming and if Doctor Braddock finds you worse, I shall be reprimanded."

"Let me catch anyone reprimanding you, beautiful. You didn't tell me your name yet, but I can make up plenty that suit," he went on audaciously.

"My name is Gaylord—Ellen Gaylord."

"Thanks. Ellen—I like that, it suits you somehow. No fuss or frills, just plain, honest-to-goodness sweetness and light." His eyelids drooped—"Good-night, Ellen—don't sneak out on me while I have forty winks, will you?" Then, after a long minute—came a sleepy—"promise?"

Ellen didn't promise and crept out when the day nurse relieved her. She liked Terry Morley just as she had liked Mrs. Langham, and as she had at first liked Violet Terrill. However, they were from another world entirely. One she had no desire to enter.

What was on Doctor Dent's mind that was so important? She dreaded going to his room, but she had promised and of course she would have to go.

CHAPTER THIRTEEN

ELLEN KEPT HER promise to drop in on Cyrus Dent that afternoon and she knew an unholy satisfaction when, upon entering, she found that Doctor Fielding and Ann Murdock were there and had the air of intending to remain for some little time. They were munching chocolates and Ann had one of the red rosebuds from a huge bouquet that stood on his dresser. Fielding and Ann were ribbing each other as was usual when the two met and when Ellen entered Cy was gleefully applauding by slapping his knee with his right hand. However, he insisted that Ellen and he had an important subject to discuss and asked them to leave.

Young Fielding groaned a refusal and settled deeper in one of the easy chair the room afforded, while Ann grinned and winked at Ellen.

"Want her consent, Doc?" she asked.

"Clever gal!" Cy was startled, his face flushed and he laughed to cover his confusion.

"Oh, save your blushes, me lad," Ann jeered, enjoying his embarrassment and Ellen's bright flare of anger. "I merely meant her consent to your annexing Lady X, lock, stock and strawberry leaves, permanent and *in toto.*"

"Some other time, Doctor Dent," Ellen said coldly, not looking at him; and before he could protest, she had fled, followed by Ann's malicious laughter. At the moment she detested Ann Murdock—despised jolly young Doctor Fielding but most of all she hated Cyrus Dent.

Ellen quite expected another midnight visit from Cy but told herself that she was relieved when he did not come. Terry Morley found her rather poor company that night and grumpily decided he might as well get some sleep. He was much improved and Ellen found she liked him better the longer she knew him. He had received a special delivery letter that morning from his sister, urging him to come home to convalesce. Ellen told him it was a grand idea especially as the hospital needed his room. So, reluctantly, but assuring Ellen he would see her as soon as he returned, he left at the end of the week. And on the day he left, Ellen received the most expensive box of candy of her life and a huge box of fragrant white lilacs—in March!

"Now, there's a patient in a millon," Marcella Harris cried, helping herself from the box of sweets. "One to restore one's belief in the innate goodness of man. You were lucky, Ellen. Ball got roses only and the day girls candy."

"Oh, I suppose it's because I took care of Lady X," Ellen explained indifferently. "She's his cousin, you know."

"Better hide that candy if you expect to find any left in the morning, darling," the older nurse advised, reaching for a gilt wrapped confection.

"Let the girls have it," Ellen said generously. "They share with me. Here, I'll leave a note." She scribbled a message and tucked it under the ribbon on the box. "Have a good time, girls. You're quite welcome."

It was a bitter night in March and Ellen drew her cape closely about her slim body as she ran across the space between the Nurses' Home and the hospital. Snow swirled about her and settled on her soft brown hair and on the tiny cap that perched there. She lifted her face to the wind. March! Even with the thermometer at zero and the wind blowing straight from Medicine Hat, she felt spring just around the corner.

Ellen was back in her favorite spot—Ward L, and the patients were once more happy. No one else seemed to know instinctively, like Nurse Gaylord, that a hot water bottle would feel good on an aching knee or that an extra pillow brought comfort to the small of one's back. No one had just the right word, grave or gay, as she had. No other nurse greeted them each time they called with the cheery smile that brown-eyed Nightingale did. They picked up the name from Doctor Dent who had been overheard so to call her. And while they didn't dare mention it to her, they talked about it among themselves, and wished the young doctor and their favorite nurse would stop this everlasting bickering and get down to business. For anyone with half an eye could see they were just made for each other.

Mary Trent, on duty with her, was cramming for a quiz. On the way up from dinner, Ann had passed Ellen on the stairs. Ellen had not been very cordial. There had been no need for that fresh jibe Ann had made that day in Dent's room. Ellen felt sure that Doctor Dent had been seriously annoyed for she had seen nothing of him since. Not that she cared, she assured herself firmly. She was glad of it, but just the same—

Now as she sat opposite Mary at the table in the alcove, she wondered just what Ann had meant by her remark as she passed her. She was carrying a tall glass—probably lime and orange juice—and had given her a crooked smile as she hurried by.

"Beyond my wildest dreams, sweetheart," she had said softly. "Just keep your fingers crossed a little while longer and I'll have the whole thing sewed up tighter than a drum."

The ward was quiet except for an occasional paroxysm of coughing. Ellen's pen paused and she leaned back in her chair, her thoughts on Ann. It would be like her to do some outlandish, crazy stunt that she would regret all her life. She had been leading up to just such a climax ever since Christmas when Tip Waring had failed her. She thought of Bill Munson as she had last seen him weeks before he came to the hospital. Small, thin and decidedly neurotic — given to long cigarette holders, checked suits, pearl gray spats and a cane. Was it possible that Ann had wangled an offer of marriage out of him? Ellen shuddered. Ann might be crazy and at times quite impossible, but she was lovely to look at and charming when she so desired.

However, Bill Munson was wealthy and Ann demanded wealth in a husband. She had said Tip and Cyrus Dent were too infantile. Well, the same couldn't be said for Bill Munson who was sixty if he was a day, and not an attractive sixty either.

Ellen picked up her pen and wrote a line or two before she laid it down again. She was very tired. Three months of night duty with the exception of one week on day work. Well, thank goodness, there was to be just one week more and she would have four long days free. She felt that she would sleep the whole time. Yes, she would go to Deacon's Landing to Aunt Bess. There, she would have rest and quiet —that's all they had there at this time of the year.

Determinedly she took up her pen, finished her letter to her mother and sent it down the mail chute. She had written that she would spend her rest period with Aunt Bess. After all, she was a nurse—her duty was to take care of the sick and she must keep well and strong for that work— "to practice my profession faithfully." Ann and Cy Dent might scoff at that pledge as they would, to Ellen it was still as sacred as the taking of vows would have been if she were of different religious faith. Just why she had hesitated before deciding she didn't stop to analyze. Nor why she felt that she would like to remain at the Nurses' Home. Certainly there would have been little chance of complete rest and quiet there with girls popping in at all hours.

She had not caught so much as a glimpse of Doctor Dent since that afternoon when she had gone to his room. That he was still confined to the hospital she knew, but he must be up and around now.

She answered a summons to the ward and returned to find Marcella Harris and her midnight lunch coming down the corridor. Marcy was always full of the latest news. Just now she was smiling enigmatically. Mary Trent reached for a sandwich as Marcella put down the tray.

"Well, spill it," she urged.

"Know what, girls? Doctor Maltby-Tipton from Denver is holding a clinic here in about ten days' time. And know why? Seventy-seven's mother has consented to an operation. We all thought that of course Mac would do it if and when she gave in, but it seems money's no object and the great Maltby-Tipton is the man of the hour. I wouldn't miss it for a king's ransom. That lad's lucky if he only knew it."

"Is the Fisher boy—Tony Fisher, in the hospital, Marcy?" Ellen asked. This was news to her.

"Sure, he's here. Came two days ago."

"So Mrs. Fisher has consented at last," Ellen said, relief in her voice. "That poor boy has died a thousand deaths in the past six years. I wonder what made her change her mind. She was as immovable as Gibraltar the last I heard."

Marcella lowered her voice to a mere whisper. "Attempted suicide—and personally, I can't blame him. Think of being a stone slab for perhaps forty or fifty years! That's why they brought him here—protection."

"I'm glad he's going to have at least a chance," Ellen murmured sympathetically.

"Do you know him?" Marcella asked curiously.

"Oh, I've heard about him—the accident on the football field and his long, heroic fight. Who hasn't?"

Her mind travelled back to that bitter night several weeks before when Doctor MacGowan had taken her to see Tony Fisher. Both Mac and his colleague, Doctor Martin, were heartsick over the mother's stubbornness in refusing an operation. It was serious, of course. Neither surgeon belittled the danger; but it was the only answer if Tony ever was to walk again. The boy was twenty—a tall, slender young fellow with a splendid head and a winning smile even in his suffering. Ellen fell in love with him at once. His mother, her lips set in stubborn lines and her eyes alert for possible trickery, watched them every minute of their stay though what she thought they could do, puzzled Ellen.

On the way back to the hospital, Ellen asked about the accident that had made Tony Fisher a cripple.

"Your barbarous game called football," the doctor told her. "Aye, an' his mither sae proud o' his valor."

"Poor thing!" murmured Ellen.

But Doctor MacGowan was bitter in his denunciation of Tony's mother.

"Selfish creature!" he muttered. "Mither love! Bah!"

"Well, isn't it?" Ellen asked. Surely the devotion Tony's mother lavished upon him proved it.

"Absolutely not," Doctor MacGowan almost shouted. "It's love of self—it's egoism. She's afraid of the pain she will suffer—afraid she will lose him."

"But, isn't that the way of most mothers? Can one blame her for that?"

"Yes. One can. I can. Oh, she's not so much afraid he might die, though perhaps that does enter into it, remotely; but she's afraid, most of all, that if he recovers he'll no longer be entirely hers. Now he is, d'ye see? As a normal young man he will no doot—doubt fall in love and wed. She will lose him much more fully then than if death took him from her. If he died she would at least be able to sit beside his grave and enjoy the luxury of weeping. Puir laddie!" he muttered.

Ellen said nothing and he went on bitterly. "The lad's faither would hae consented I hae na doot. It's a peety when a lad is left wi' only a mither—especially a mither who is sic a gowk." The doctor became very Scotch when excited or upset and now his r's rolled delightfully. Ellen wished he would go on talking. "Martin's na fule—he's workin' wi—with her to have him brought to Anthony Ware. After that—we'll see." He turned to smile down at her. "Not an especially pleasant journey this night, eh, Miss Ellen?"

"Oh, but it was—that is, I liked meeting Tony, and I do hope we can help him. After all, Doctor MacGowan, the chances are all in his favor. You have done the operation successfully several times before, haven't you?"

"Ah, but I'll not be doing the operating," he muttered, and Ellen felt sure his voice held deep hurt. "It's the old story: a prophet is not without honor, save in his ain countra, and I've been at Anthony Ware just long enough for Mrs. Fisher to feel the contempt of familiarity. An expert, you know, is always a man from out of town. No, my lass, we'll get Maltby-Tipton from Denver. He's her choice. But the battle is nae ours yet, lass. We'll hae t'bide oor time. Martin's a clever one, though."

They were nearing Brentwood. The doctor gave a deep sigh and straightened at the wheel as if he were sloughing off the worries that were riding him. His smile was charming as he turned his head to look down at her.

"This trip hasn't accomplished what I hoped it would, Miss Gaylord. I had an idea we should become better acquainted. With your permission we'll try it again some time soon, shall we?"

"Thank you," Ellen murmured, her heart racing. Just what did he mean by that? she wondered. She felt a little shiver of distaste. No, it would never do if, as Ann insisted, Mac was becoming interested in her.

She recalled how gently he helped her from his car and how solicitous in regard to the warmth of her coat. His hand brushed her cheek lightly as he fitted her key into the lock at the Nurses' Home.

"Sleep well, lass. I'm glad you are blessed with health as well as beauty and common sense. Not often does the gude Lord so lavishly endow mortals. Be thankful to Him. Good night, and thank you for accompanying me."

Ellen had not yet made that second trip, in fact, she had seen little of Doctor MacGowan since the epidemic had been with them. She wondered that Mrs. Fisher had consented to have Tony brought to the hospital during the siege. Probably, though, he would be safer here than at home. Somehow Tony didn't seem like a boy who would attempt suicide.

"Did you hear what he did?" Ellen asked.

"Took an overdose of some sedative his doctor had left. Laura Coggswell's his nurse, you know, and she said his mother was frantic and blamed her for negligence. However, both Doctor Martin and Tony defended her, and really, Ellen, I think there's something kind of phony about that story. Coggswell wasn't much concerned and neither was Martin. They informed the mother he would no doubt try it again as long as his case remained hopeless —or something of the sort. He's in seventy-seven—Mrs. Fisher believes the numeral seven brings luck or something. Anyway, she insisted on a room with a seven in it. She's a nut!"

"Is Coggswell coming with him?" Mary asked.

"She is not. Ma Fisher's all washed up with her. And of course, Anthony Ware nurses aren't swanky enough to suit the lady, so Miss Booth and a Miss Nelson are adding lustre to our lives and I feel sorry for the kid—they're both over forty and ugly as sin, but my deahs! Are they ritzy! I suppose Ma Fisher was afraid her darling might fall in love with one of our girls. At that, he might do a whole lot worse."

"Pooh!" scoffed Mary Trent, setting down her empty cup. "Who, in her right mind, would take on Mrs. Fisher? We kids used to visit her cook on Fridays. She's a Louisiana nigger and makes cakes that give one thoughts of Paradise. Melt in your mouth. Our place joins the Fisher land—oh, nearly a mile over the hill, but we thought nothing of sneaking cross lots on Fridays. The old dame got wise to us after a while and set one of the gardeners on us. He made a great hullabaloo while she was within earshot and then filled our arms with fruit and advised us to see him before we staged another raid. She's an old pill!" A dreamy look came into her eyes. "Tony's a peach—or used to be."

"Well, I'm glad he's here, Marcy." And after a moment —"Seen Ann lately? to talk to, I mean." Ellen was still puzzled over Ann's whispered request that she keep her fingers crossed.

Marcella laughed. "Ann's wearing a particularly irritating expression these days—smug and superior, but she won't talk. North's on her case days, and she say she never had a more disagreeable patient. I can't make Ann out. Every afternoon she goes for a walk—alone, mind you, instead of going to the gym as she used to. Yesterday, she brought back a brief case. An errand for Munson, I imagine; but can you feature Ann Murdock running errands for anyone, even a wealthy patient, unless, of course, she expects to get something out of it. But Munson!" Marcella shook her head. "Surely not Munson!"

"No," Ellen repeated with conviction—"not Munson!"

Ellen was restless after Marcella went down stairs. She went through the ward, eyeing each patient solicitously. Extra beds had been brought in and every one was occupied. Little Angela Dubail had gone on just a week before and a small, be-earringed old lady with pleurisy and a bad knee, was in the place she had once occupied. But she was no charity patient, the old lady assured those who would listen. Her son, Michael was paying good money for her. Now she opened bright dark eyes and stared at Ellen.

"Hist!" she whispered sibilantly. "That hussy down at the end's a bad 'un. Watch out for her."

Ellen patted her hand and smiled down at the wrinkled face. "Don't worry, Mrs. Connors. Just go to sleep and everything will be fine. You'll soon be better."

"Better, is it? Not while I hev t' breathe th' same dirty air as that one. She's no good, I tell you."

Her eyes glared at the last bed whose occupant seemed sleeping quietly except for an occasional cough. Then she jerked to a sitting position and pointed a long, bony finger. "There she is, th' she-devil! I'll cut her heart out!" Her hoarse voice was still low but any minute Ellen knew she might become loud and violent. She punched the button at the head of her bed and Mary Trent hurried in.

"Call Doctor Braddock while I quiet her," Ellen whispered.

However, it wasn't Braddock who answered the summons, but Cyrus Dent, his arm still in a sling. Ellen wondered what he thought he could do with one arm. But it seemed Mrs. Connors had great respect for the male sex and lay down at his suggestion.

"Give her a hypo," he prescribed as Ellen settled the old woman beneath the blankets. "This isn't any too good for her." He slipped a thermometer beneath her tongue and at the sly look in her eyes, he warned. "Don't you dare bite that or—" He didn't finish, just warned her with his eyes. She didn't bite it and after a moment he reported that it wasn't temperature so much as temperament. "The lady wants attention, I'm thinking, Nightingale," he grinned and Ellen's heart suddenly warmed at the old teasing tone.

"She seems to have it in for Tessie Sheeshan, down at the end. Poor girl, I'm sure she's anything but a hussy." Ellen lingered beside the bed until Mrs. Connors slept. Doctor Dent followed her out into the corridor. "How's the shoulder?" Ellen asked, with kindly solicitude.

"Coming along slowly. It's a heck of a time to be laid up, with all this sickness. Braddock's just plain worn out and I told him I'd take his place from midnight on. How's life using you these days—or nights?" His tone was light, friendly, and Ellen felt somewhat lost. Here she had been building up to a frigid hauteur when next she should meet him, and he was as friendly and non-combative as a two-year-old. "What do you hear from Terry Morley?" he asked suddenly and Ellen caught her breath.

"O-oh," she said, "you startled me. I had forgotten for a moment that—"

"I was here?" he laughed.

"Oh, I'm tired, I guess. My thoughts were miles away. Terry Morley? I don't know. I haven't heard."

"You haven't? I'm surprised. His sister thinks he is quite impressed with your ability and—er—pulchritude."

"His sister? Oh, Mrs. Langham. I had forgotten." He must think I'm either a moron or an awful liar, she thought to herself. "How is she and how is Lady Violet?"

"Wonderful!" he said heartily. "By the way, how was it that they didn't know you donated your blood first—days before mine was used?"

"I haven't the least idea. Lady Violet wasn't particularly interested in me—or perhaps she forgot; but it doesn't matter. I don't mind. Is—is Mr. Morely still in Boston?" she asked after a moment.

"He was the last I heard. But no doubt he'll be back soon. Good looking chap, isn't he?"

"Wonderful!" Ellen was suddenly enthusiastic. "And nice, too. So thoughtful and—and pleasant."

"Ye-ah! It sort of runs in the family—that sweet disposition. Grand to have a good disposition!" Abruptly, Doctor Dent turned and strode away.

It wasn't until the next afternoon that Ellen heard just why Mrs. Connors had such a hatred for Tessie Sheehan. Marcella Harris, who knew everything, told her that Michael Connors was sweet on Tessie and the old lady was afraid she would lose his pay envelope. Michael was a good son—a dutiful son. Mother Connors had enjoyed the spending of most of Michael's weekly wage for many years. Michael had never noticed girls until little Tessie Sheehan moved into their block.

Apparently, it was love at first sight for both of them. Inez Dostevski brought wild tales of what was going on to Michael's mother and the old woman set about putting a stop to all that sort of nonsense.

Ellen saw Inez as she was leaving the next evening and thought she knew the cause of Mrs. Connors' enmity. Mike was with her—a worried, brow-beaten look on his broad, ruddy face. Inez, clinging to his arm, was comforting him with soft cluckings of the tongue, her black eyes covetous. Ellen watched them out of sight. So that was it! It was none of her business, of course, only as it affected the welfare of a patient. Well, this did. Tessie Sheehan looked beaten —lost.

"Good evening, Mrs. Connors!" Ellen greeted the sick woman when she entered the ward. "So that was your son, Michael? A fine, strapping young fellow, isn't he? How is it, I wonder, that good, dependable men like Mike so often fall in love with girls like the one he was with. I understand they are engaged and that you don't approve. Well, Mrs. Connors, I can't altogether blame you."

Mrs. Connors glared at her. "Mike ain't engaged to that girl. He don't even like her."

"He doesn't! You must be mistaken—they—well, she certainly likes him. Too bad, isn't it? Maybe you can do a little match-making there, Mrs. Connors. Mothers are clever in picking out the proper wives for their boys, I understand. You like that girl, don't you? I'm afraid I ought not to have said what I did that—"

"Like Inez Dostevski? Oh, she's well enough as far as that goes. She's a good worker, Inez is, but she's years older 'n Mike." She frowned darkly and muttered to herself.

"Yes, I could see that, but nevertheless I could see that she is crazy about him. Oh, well, probably Mike can take care of himself. Only, Mrs. Connors," Ellen's voice became confidential, "if you don't want that Inez for a daughter-in-law, better watch out. If ever I saw a predatory look in a female's eyes, it was in hers as they left this room."

"An' what kind of a look might that be, Nurse?" Mrs. Connors asked, worriedly.

"Oh, just that she'd like to have him for a husband, or, maybe just for her beau. Now, how do you feel this evening? I hope you are lots better and will soon be able to go home and look after Mike yourself. What you needs is some strong, pleasant young girl to help you. I'll speak to your son. Maybe he could prevail upon some girl to come in and stay with you until your knee is entirely well."

"We ain't millionaires, Nurse," the old woman muttered.

"Oh, it won't cost much—maybe a couple of dollars a day."

"A couple of—"

"Don't worry, Mrs. Connors. You will be here for another week at least. Maybe when you get home you will have a daughter and won't need a maid." Ellen smiled down at her. She could see the idea seeping through her brain. She didn't know that Mike had used that same argument when his mother hurt her knee. Tessie had insisted that his mother live with them so she could look after her.

"So that's her game," she muttered as Ellen walked on down the ward. Scarcely an hour later, Ellen answered her impatient summons.

"How's she gettin' along, Nurse?" She pointed a long bony finger at the bed occupied by Tessie Sheehan, but now her eyes were merely curious — no longer belligerent.

"She's been pretty sick, but she's a strong young thing and will be out before we know it. Such a sweet girl with a true Irish sense of humor. A little like you, Mrs. Connors. Honest and generous and well—just grand! I like the Irish —they're so straight and—well—aboveboard. Did you ever know an Irishman do a mean, underhanded trick, Mrs. Connors?"

The black eyes twinkled. "You've a drop o' Irish blood in yer own veins I'm thinkin', Nurse. Yis, we're all alike—us Irish. Give that little hussy down there my regards, an' tell her I'll have me son, Michael, bring her some oranges tomorrah."

Ellen moved to the bed of little Tessie Sheehan and delivered her message. Tessie gasped and her eyes, so dull and hopeless, suddenly brightened. She smiled at the be-earringed old woman and weakly lifted a hand in salute.

"So you see, Tessie, you must hurry and get well. Maybe you can beat Mrs. Connors home and have dinner all ready so that she'll think you're the best housekeeper in the world."

"You knew?" Tessie's black-lashed blue eyes glowed into Ellen's. "But Inez was so horrid—"

"Forget Inez, by dear. She's completely out of the picture and you see that she stays out. Hear me?"

"I will!" Tessie's small chin was out-thrust and she clenched her fist. "If Mike's mother's on our side I'm not afraid of anything Inez can do. Oh, you're a darling, Miss Gaylord! I don't wonder everyone loves you. I do, myself," she added, shyly.

CHAPTER FOURTEEN

IT WAS A WEEK later that Ann Murdock came into Ellen's room just as that young lady was dressing to go out. Always lovely, Ann was particularly radiant this afternoon, with the hard brilliance of polished metal. She flung herself down on Ellen's bed with a sigh of smug satisfaction.

"Well, old dear, the deed is done—I landed him. He was wary at first and inclined to be suspicious; but the bait was tempting—so completely honest—so subtly naive and alluring, you know, that he nibbled, then bit, then gulped and presto! I had him hooked!" Ann made all the gestures of an angler trying to capture a particularly wily game fish.

Ellen laughed in spite of herself, then gasped as Ann held up her left hand on which glittered a diamond of impressive size.

"But—but Ann—you're not engaged!"

"Nothing else but, darling," she said complaisantly. "You see, I was taking no chances of his slipping off my hook. Breach of promise isn't a pretty combination of words."

"Don't be vulgar, Ann," Ellen exclaimed impatiently. "I hate it." An unpleasant thought seeped through the amazement. "I don't think I understand about this," she said after a moment. "You surely can't be in love with Munson."

"Munson!" shrieked Ann, sitting up abruptly. "Are you crazy? Think I'd ever marry that old fossil, Ellen Gaylord?"

"Well, you said—then who—"

"Why, Jim Ellis, to be sure," Ann said airily.

"Jim Ellis! And who in the world may Jim Ellis be? I never heard of him."

"You have too. Jim Ellis is old Munson's nephew and heir. He's here in the paper mill while old Bill is laid up. They hate each other like poison, but each finds the other necessary to the success of the paper business. Jim is sales manager. His offices are in New York. Oh, New York!" Ann rolled her eyes ecstatically.

"I think I do remember a nephew somewhere," Ellen said. "Sort of a queer—I don't think I ever saw him, though," she finished hastily.

"Oh, as to that, you haven't missed much, my lamb," Ann grinned, then wrinkled her nose childishly. "A poor thing, but mine own, don't you know. He's not much to look at, but thank heaven, he's tall and isn't addicted to spats—the rest I intend to improve or else—" She paused and watched the light play on the stone in her ring. "What's more to the point, my child, he's got what it takes —money!"

"If you are trying to shock me, Ann Murdock—" Ellen began.

"And why should I try to shock you, sweetheart?" Ann purred.

"—it's quite useless. I'm not a bit shocked. You're probable madly in love with this man and are just putting on an act for my benefit."

Ann stared at her friend for a moment with hard, bright eyes, then her face softened. "Oh, Jim's not half bad, Ellen, that is—well, he's a whole lot better than some men I could mention. I imagine he'll never let me down. He's a good sort—an understanding soul and seems quite mad about me." She took off her ring and slipped it into the pocket of the knitted dress she was wearing.

"But—Ann, do you—you do love him, don't you?" Ellen's voice was worried.

"Love him?" Ellen had a sudden picture of Ann at Christmas when news reached her of Tip Waring's engagement to another girl. Ann, her face crumpled, all the hardness gone. "But Ellen, I like Tip—rather a lot!" Ann had been different since that time. Ellen saw that she was much thinner, too, and inclined to nervousness. "I don't believe in love," Ann said with a brittle laugh.

"Oh, Ann!"

"We're keeping it dark until Uncle Bill—don't you just love that 'Uncle,' Ellen? Until old Bill Munson gets out of here. We don't want to stage a scene in this place. Jim's going to tell him on the day we leave for New York. Oh, New York!" she sighed again.

"And when are you going to—"

Ann laughed. "Still the same old Stiff-in-the-morals, aren't you?" she jeered. "I intend making an honest man of him, my child, never fear. We already have the license, just in case. Oh, everything is going to be according to Hoyle. I won't go until after the wedding, I promise."

"Miss Forsyth will be annoyed—"

Ann laughed again. "A lot I care for old Ag. or any of the rest of the vegetables in this place. If she hadn't been so soft it never would have happened," she said fiercely. "But no, she sent me to Munson—the rest was just fate. Don't look so bewildered, infant. And haven't you forgotten something? Aren't you glad for me? Aren't you going to wish me happiness?" she finished, her eyes mocking.

Ellen sat down on the bed beside her visitor and searched the black-lashed green eyes beneath the mass of wavy red hair. After a moment in which she read nothing but mockery, she slowly shook her head. "I hope you'll be happy, Ann," she said softly as she kissed her, "but I wish you wouldn't—"

Ann drew away from that kiss. "Happy?" she repeated slowly, then sat erect, her chin out-thrust. "Of course I'll be happy—I intend to be. But listen, not one word of this to a soul. Old Bill won't be discharged for another two weeks and it will be a month at least before we can get out of this burg."

The girls parted. After a while of troubled thought, Ellen let the matter slip completely from her mind. Doctor Braddock was down with pneumonia and the hospital walked on tiptoe, for the fat little House Physician was universally beloved. Miss Forsyth went about with eyes from which the light had departed. Mac growled his orders and grew thin and hollow-eyed from loss of sleep. Fielding and Dent were on duty twenty-four hours of the day and every nurse slipped about on silent, white-shod feet, valiantly fighting with the little doctor who was alike their source of comfort and amusement.

It was the fifth day of Dr. Braddock's illness. He lay in an oxygen tent, apparently fighting a losing battle. MacGowan walked the corridor outside and Ellen who passed him there saw his lips move and knew that he prayed to his stern, just, Scotch Presbyterian God to spare his colleague's life. A block away, Emilie, Doctor Braddock's spoiled, selfish, neurotic wife, eluded her nurse and wandered away to be found two hours later in the river.

It was days after the doctor was convalescent before he was told of the tragedy. And it wasn't until he was able to sit up, irritable and demanding, that his nurse, Mary Burns, who never missed a trick, but who was splendid in pneumonia cases, told the other nurses in strictest confidence that his first conscious words were: "Agatha—darling!"

"And if I dared I'd tell the poor thing," she told them. "To think of their loving each other all these years! I think it's beautiful. I suppose, though, it's a little soon to—"

Ann laughed. "Emilie's as dead as she ever will be."

No one said anything. One by one they left the room and Ann turned to Ellen with a crooked grin.

"They think I'm a hussy, don't they, angel?"

"It's your own fault if they do, Ann," Ellen reminded her. "You've completely sold yourself to them in that role and your can't blame them for believing it's the real you."

"And one might as well have the game as the name, eh? I intend being hard and selfish and acquisitive from now on. God helps those who help themselves, I've found, and the devil makes a monkey out of the hindmost. No one is going to make a monkey out of me—ever again."

A maid came to Ellen's door and knocked softly.

"Is Miss Murdock—Oh, there's a gentleman downstairs. He asked for you, Miss Murdock. Shall I tell him you'll be down?"

"I'll tell him myself, thanks, Jean. Come on, Ellen. It's Jim. I want you to meet him. He's no great beauty and he's not so young, but at that he's not so bad and all in all—"

"Oh, shut up, Ann," Ellen said sharply. "You make me sick. I feel like forbidding the banns or something."

They entered the long reception room side by side. A tall man was striding up and down—his mouth set in a grim, stubborn line. Ann paused just inside the door—gasped, then gave a shrill little cry.

"Tip!"

Ellen felt she knew the reason for Ann's contemplated precipitate marriage. With a muttered exclamation, the man rushed to meet her and she was in his arms, sobbing wildly. Ellen stood for a moment utterly bewildered, then slipped quietly away. What had Ann done!

Ann didn't come to dinner and Ellen didn't see her again that night. It was Marcella Harris who brought her news of the collapse of Ann.

"Maybe you don't think there was the very deuce to pay," Marcella said, her eyes shining with excitement.

"Where on earth did Ann ever meet that Ellis creature in the first place? He doesn't live here. This Tip and she have always been sweethearts, haven't they? But wasn't there something about her girl friend cutting her out, or what was it? Do you know, Ellen?"

Ellen looked blank.

"Then, why did she want this Ellis? Money, I suppose."

"If you ask me, I'd say Ann Murdock is getting just what she deserves," little Mary Trent said sharply. "She just about the freshest thing I've ever seen, and hard-boiled as they come."

Remembering Ann's face on Christmas Eve, Ellen didn't agree. "Ann's manner is just protective coloring, girls," she told them. "Actually, she's terribly sensitive, with a bad inferiority complex. She's hard and pert to cover it up."

"Maybe," Marcella conceded, "but it was a crazy thing for her to do. Get engaged on impulse like that and to a man of his type. She can't possibly know him and if he's anything like his uncle—God help her!"

"Crazy? Sure it was," Mary Trent had never liked Ann and had no sympathy for her now. "How does Forsyth feel about it? Did you hear?"

"No. And what's more, we won't hear. Lately Agatha and Ann have been just like that." Marcella held up her hand, the first two fingers pressed close together, "and knowing Ann, it looks mighty fishy to me."

"Where is Ann, now?" Ellen asked. "Not on duty, of course."

"I'll say she's not. She went completely haywire all over the house and this Tip got scared and rang for Mrs. Drake who promptly called a doctor—MacGowan went, and they put her to bed over in the room Dent had. Fielding and he haven't been having much use for beds lately. She was raving the last I knew and when the Ellis man came and demanded he be allowed to see her, Ann gave one look at him and fainted again. Fine mess, if you ask me."

"Oh, I'm sorry," Ellen said. "I wonder if they will let me see her. I wish—"

"You needn't waste any sympathy on Ann Murdock," Marcella advised crisply. "I reckon she got what she set out to get—a rich husband and if you want my opinion, Anthony Ware will be lots better off without her, for she's always creating some sort of disturbance."

"Just the same, I'm sorry," Ellen repeated.

"Well, I guess you're the only one who is," Marcella insisted. "Even Angus called her a 'jillet,' full of 'joukery-pawkery'—at least that's what it sounded like and I imagine they're not exactly terms of affectionate regard. They sound pretty awful to me. You knew he refused to work with her lately, didn't you? On operations, I mean. Sort of got in his hair, no doubt."

Ellen didn't know and wondered if MacGowan had discovered about the Symphony Concert tickets. Poor Ann! She wished she could go to her now. She would surely see her before she left for her four days respite at Deacon's Landing.

It was shortly before dinner next afternoon that Tip Waring waited for her in the long reception room.

"You are Ann's best friend, Miss Gaylord—she talked a lot about you. Tell me about this man she has mixed herself up with. How did it happen?"

"Why, you must know how and why it happened much better than I do, Mr. Waring—Tip," Ellen told him. "Were you and Ann ever actually engaged?"

"Not officially, if that's what you mean. We've always gone around together and both of us understood—at least I did—that some day when I got through law school we'd marry. I was all for marrying first. I never wanted Ann to become a nurse in the first place. We could have made a go of it somehow. But Ann felt she would only hinder me and in order not to be a burden any longer on her family, decided to enter a training school where she could at least earn her 'keep' as she called it. She used to say she'd make a much better wife and mother, too, with that extra training. Oh, Ellen, she's such a grand girl! Brave and smiling when I know she'd much rather hide off in a corner somewhere and bawl. You see, I know Ann. I guess you do, too."

"Yes." Ellen said soberly. "I think I do."

"Well I finished law school and then the man who had promised to take me in with him, died suddenly. I tried a dozen different offices with no luck. At last I decided to go it alone and work at odd jobs until things picked up. Well," his face flushed and his eyes shifted in embarrassment. "I went to Marge Horton's father's mill to help with the auditing. It was just before Christmas. I hate to tell this, Miss —Ellen. It sounds sort of caddish but it's the truth. I shall always feel that she engineered the whole thing. Why, Lord only knows. Surely I'm no great catch for any girl to lose her head over. Anyway—Oh, skip it. First thing I knew, Marge was telling the family that we were engaged, and the old folks were making a fuss over me and Marge was crying and laughing. From that time on I tried to get out of it. I guess I'm no gentleman, Ellen. I didn't want Marge. And then Ann returned all my letters unopened. I was frantic. I even came on here to see her but she refused to see me. Did you know that?

"When the news of her engagement to this Ellis man came I told Marge plainly that I was through. I didn't care what scandal developed. I was going to see Ann and tell her the rights of the whole affair. Ellen, she looks terrible. She's sick!"

"I know, Tip. I think Ann was dreadfully hurt when she heard that you were marrying her best friend. I know she hasn't been the same since. Tip, you can't let her go on with this marriage. You must do something."

"I intend to. But if she really cares for this man, what then?"

"She can't. Don't give her up, Tip."

"I won't and I want you to help me. Make her see my side of it. Stick to her and to me."

Ellen didn't have the heart to tell him that day after next she was leaving for Deacon's Landing to be gone four whole days.

CHAPTER FIFTEEN

BUT ELLEN WAS destined not to go to Deacon's Landing just yet. Ann kept calling for Tip—calling incessantly. Tip was sent for and sat close by, her hand tight in his, as he crooned softly to her. At last, she seemed to arouse and he took her in his arms and held her close. Agatha Forsyth, tired and worn from the strain of the past hectic weeks, had taken almost complete charge of her. Every nurse in Anthony Ware was doing double duty, and the Superintendent loved Ann.

MacGowan was troubled. It was a bad mess, especially as Bill Munson was making a fuss about it all upstairs. The old man couldn't kick his nephew out because the business was in trust, but he could refuse to see either him or the little gold-digger who had ensnared him. He blamed the hospital for harboring such creatures and raved at his unoffending nurse until the girl was close to tears and, mentally, threatened to quit.

And it was, strangely enough, MacGowan himself who put the old man in his place and talked to him as no doubt he had never been talked to before. And all this time, Jim Ellis was in a blue funk. He hadn't wanted to fall in love with the girl in the first place—girls didn't interest him—never had; but she was such a cute, impertinent little trick that she got right under his skin and the first thing he knew she had him eating out of her hand. He wasn't in the least sorry—if she would go through with it. He intended seeing she wouldn't regret the bargain, but what about this Tip Waring? Where did he come in?

It was the day before Ellen's four days rest period began, that a call came for her to report to room forty-three at once. That was the room Doctor Dent had occupied and that Ann now had. She was shocked at Ann's appearance. How was it possible for Ann to become so emaciated and so haggard in just a few days? Ellen took Ann's hot hand in her own.

"Ann, darling, I'm so sorry."

"Stay with me, Ellen," Ann pleaded. "The nights are so —so horrible!"

"If I'm allowed to, Ann," Ellen told her and Miss Forsyth nodded her head in relief. She knew Ellen rated time off but she was young and strong—she could manage all right and would no doubt be good for Ann. Miss Forsyth was feeling the weight of her years. "I'll just run along and change into a uniform and be right back," Ellen promised.

For the first time since she entered the room, Ann smiled. Ellen hurried away. What did it matter if she was tired out or if she had planned that visit to Aunt Bess? Everyone in the hospital was tired, too, and Ann needed her.

And Ann was to need her more than ever before the night was over, for late that afternoon, Tip Waring was instantly killed when his car skidded into the concrete abutment of Brentwood River bridge. Jim Ellis, thinking no doubt to break the news to her gently, told Ann of the accident. And Ann didn't faint when he told her, she merely said with deadly calm:

"It was all a mistake, Jim. I'll see that you get your ring back. I can't go on—I thought I could, but now, I know I can't. Please go." Then, as he attempted to soothe her. "Go—go—go!" Each repetition was a little louder, a little more shrill and Ellen urged him to leave quickly.

"Ellen, Ellen, what have I done? What have I done?" Ann sobbed, burying her head in Ellen's lap. "Oh, Tip—don't leave me! Please come back to me! I love you so!"

Over and over she moaned that last until from sheer exhaustion, she slept.

But Jim Ellis wouldn't accept dismissal. And again it was Doctor MacGowan who accomplished what Ann and Ellen couldn't.

"Be a gude sport, man," he urged. "The lass is in no condition for shilly-shallying. Better a clean break—it's soonest healed. Each one of us has his Gethsemane and his Calvary—the lass is o'er young to have met hers, but the kindest thing we can do is to let a-be. Only time can heal a sair heart."

Jim Ellis said a regretful farewell to his beautiful dream. Later, he returned to New York, leaving a new Ann—a quieter Ann. All the hardness—all the smart sophistication gone.

In those first trying days, Doctor MacGowan and she became more friendly. The dour Scot took to teasing her about the loss of her temper, declaring no redhead was true to type without it. Ann would smile sadly and shake her lovely head.

"I guess I'm pretty much of a problem, Doctor. But it's just as Ellen always told me. It's mostly on the outside that I'm hard. Inside I've always been a cowardly little 'fraid-cat, shivering in terror for fear someone would snub me or hurt my pride."

"You a coward, lass?" He shook his head. "Not any more. You're a woman, now. Before, you were but a child, blundering against life with your eyes shut. Oft-times life has to chasten us sair, ere we submit tae her guidance. Ye'll be th' better for th' lesson, lass."

Ellen's brown eyes glowed when Ann repeated the conversation to her. "I always said he was grand, Ann."

Ann smiled briefly with something of her old mischief. "And I accused you of making up to him." Her eyes darkened. "Somehow, I feel years older—that I've come a long way since—since—Oh, Ellen!" The lovely face twisted in an agony of regret. "Tip!" she whispered. "Oh, Tip!"

And Ellen, her heart torn with compassion, could do little but hold her close in her strong young arms until the paroxysm of weeping had subsided and drawing away, Ann attempted a smile that was sadder than tears.

"I'm a mess, Ellen," she apologized. "I'm ashamed of being such a weak sister, but—but—"

"You weak, Ann!" scoffed Ellen hastily. "I don't think even your worst enemy could ever call you weak. You're just human and—and—"

"I know," Ann interrupted, "but I killed Tip Waring, Ellen. If I hadn't been such a crazy, headstrong fool—"

"No," Ellen protested. "It just had to be that Tip should die, but his love, Ann," Ellen said softly, "his love didn't die. Nothing can kill that. You will always have his love —always—"

Ann's eyes filled again. "I know, but it's Tip—Tip himself, I need. His arms about me—his dear presence and now—"

"Now, he's nearer than ever. He'll never fail you again, Ann. Never let you down. All through your life you will know that his love surrounds you—a warm, protecting shelter from every sorrow and hardship that may come to you. Darling, you must believe me. Love is stronger than death, Ann. It doesn't die."

Ann lay quiet for a long moment while Ellen's gentle words seemed vibrant in the stillness. Her eyes had the far-away look of one trying to pierce the veil that hangs between the two worlds. At last, with a long shuddering sigh, the heavy lids closed and soon she slept.

From that time on, Ann showed steady improvement and was soon able to sit up. The nurses made short duty-calls to her room, curious to see the heroine of the tragic though thrilling romance. They talked about it among themselves.

"She's changed," Thompson said one late afternoon as they lingered in Ellen's room. "All the old sparkle and pep are gone."

"Well, what did you expect?" Marcella Harris asked sharply, unexpectedly allying herself with Ann whom she had never really liked.

"Don't worry. Murdock hasn't changed permanently," Isabelle Hess offered, a wary eye on Ellen. "Remember, 'when the devil was sick, the devil a saint would be, but— when the devil got well, devil a saint was he!' That's Ann Murdock, or I miss my guess. Can a leopard change his spots or—or" she added quickly, noting Ellen's sudden defensive gesture, "Mac his disposition?"

There was a general laugh. Only yesterday Hess had been rudely awakened from a day-dream by the rasping burr of the Chief of Staff who had been compelled to repeat a request—an unheard of occurrence, even in the scrub room, where attending nurses vied with each other in service to their chief. The story had spread and gathered color and burrs on its journey.

"Every 'r-r' felt like a bullet str-r-r-iking me," Hess grumbled, "and I—I dead on my feet!"

"And next time I'll let you ring the bell, my lady," Mary Burns warned. "Three o'clock!"

"Hess out until three!" chorused the others. "Who— where—"

"Oh, Hess' big moment is the little dentist over on Chapel Street," Marcella Harris, who knew everything, told them. "But three o'clock!"

"Well, what's wrong with three o'clock?" Hess wanted to know. "Anything immoral about three o'clock? Seems to me there's a song about three o'clock."

"Oh, yeah! Well, maybe it's not immoral exactly," Burns muttered darkly, "but it's darned inconsiderate. I couldn't get back to sleep after I hauled you in from the fire escape."

"Hauled, is right. I tore my new dress on that darned window. Don't I have the worst luck?" the culprit mourned.

"Nothing to what you will have if it happens again, my friend," she was warned.

"Oh, you!" was all the answer Hess made.

Marcella Harris turned to Ellen who sat on the floor with her head against the windowseat, her arms about her knees.

"Ann's better, isn't she?"

"Yes," Ellen answered. "She'll be all right now."

"How long are you on there?" Thompson asked.

"I'm off now. Ann's going home to convalesce. She needs a change." Ellen hoped they were not going to begin on Ann again. "I'm on call for a while, and it's to be hoped nothing very terrible happens for I can't answer for my disposition if there are too many demands upon me. I think I've never been quite so tired before."

"Nor I either," Thompson said, yawning sleepily, while Hess frankly dozed on the bed, prodded occasionally by the unsympathetic Burns. "We've had a tough time here. Thank heaven it's letting up. I wish I was going to be on the Fisher case. Anyway, I'm going to try to be there when Maltby-Tipton does his stuff. They say he's a wiz."

"He may be," Ellen agreed, "but I doubt if he's any better than Mac. Somehow—"

Isabelle Hess awoke to jeer. "Mac! I'd like to do a little operating on him."

No one paid any attention to her and she dozed again. Ellen went on:

"—I'd feel surer of the outcome if Mac was to do the job."

"Oh, you and Mac!" scoffed Thompson. "You act as if he was a tin god, Gaylord. Granted he's good—I'm not belittling him, but there are others—"

"For Pete's sake, stop arguing!" snapped Hess, burrowing into Ellen's pillow.

"And for Pete's sake get off my bed!" Ellen ordered. "It's been made once today."

The gong in the lower hall sounded. Dinner! Even Hess roused at the summons and went down with the others.

"Say, just why isn't Mac operating on young Fisher?" Marcella asked inquisitively. "After all—"

Ellen shook her head. "Don't ask me. I only know I'm going to be there if it's the last thing I do."

CHAPTER SIXTEEN

THE GREAT DOCTOR Maltby-Tipton arrived in Brentwood on the day Ann departed for home. She expressed regret that she would miss him, for his clinic would be attended by doctors and nurses from many outlying towns. Even Corinth Medical was sending its students over to watch the great man perform one of his miracles. Ellen felt a little stab of jealousy for their own Doctor MacGowan. She doubted that the Denver surgeon was in any way superior to their own Chief of Staff. It was just a case of the unappreciated prophet. However, she was keen to see the man and to watch his greatly vaunted technique.

Tony Fisher was ready and eager for the event. He was in better spirits than he had been for some time, his nurses reported, and the night before the day of the operation, he went to sleep early, even before his weeping mother had left the room.

"It's like it used to be before the big game," he told his night nurse. "We had to get to bed early so as to be ready for the battle. This is my big game, isn't it? Probably the biggest game I'll ever play. I want to be fit to meet each emergency and to win all along the line—to make a touchdown—to win!"

Mrs. Fisher was sobbing hysterically as she left his room and Doctor Martin hurried her away.

Maltby-Tipton stopped in to see the sleeping boy and Doctor Martin told him what Tony had said. The great man bit his lip.

"I don't understand why your own MacGowan doesn't do it," he said. And Doctor Martin thought the man didn't look at all well. Tired and a bit worried. He mentioned the fact to the Chief of Staff who passed over the information with the remark that the Denver surgeon was probably weary from his long trip which, disliking planes, he had made by train.

But it was only a little after one in the morning that Doctor MacGowan was called to the Durston Hotel. Doctor Maltby-Tipton was gravely ill. In half an hour the famous surgeon was on the operating table at Anthony Ware and Doctor MacGowan was performing an emergency appendectomy. Ellen was one of the nurses in attendance and felt a wave of exultation as she watched. Afterwards, as she scrubbed with the others, she was far too excited to talk. Now, Doctor MacGowan would have to operate on Tony Fisher! Now, she felt sure, the boy would recover. She hadn't been any too confident before, why, she couldn't explain. Surely Fate worked by devious methods!

Ellen, however, had reckoned without Tony's mother. The lady stubbornly refused to have anyone but Maltby-Tipton touch her boy. They left her alone with Tony when they had reached the end of their patience and when, two hours later, he rang for a nurse, Mrs. Fisher was white, exhausted and bitterly angry. Tony seemed years older.

"I'm ready," was all the boy said and after that things moved swiftly. His mother let him go without a good-bye.

Though Ellen had been on night duty and knew she should have gone to bed directly after chapel that morning, she filed into the operating theatre with the others. Only a few knew of the change in surgeons but as far as Ellen could see, there was little if any disappointment shown by those occupying seats around the small group of masked white figures under that great dome. A hushed expectancy hung over the room. The tragedy of Tony Fisher was well known in this part of the state and every person there consciously or unconsciously breathed a prayer that Mac-Gowan's God would not desert him now.

Forty minutes later, Tony was wheeled to the elevator and taken down to his room. The clinic was over—students, nurses and doctors wandered down corridors and out into the early spring sunshine. Ellen, still to excited for bed, changed into street clothes and went for a long, solitary walk. She returned two hours later and went to the Receiving Room, hoping for news.

Doctor Braddock told her that young Fisher was still under ether but his reactions were perfectly normal and there was every chance in the world that the operation was successful although one could not be sure so early in the game. Doctor Maltby-Tipton was coming along nicely and seemed greatly relieved that Tony's operation was now over. Doctor Braddock chuckled.

"Maltby-Tipton may be the man of the hour, Gaylord, I'm not belittling him one inch; but you've got to show me a greater surgeon than our own Angus MacGowan."

"So say we all!" Ellen agreed. "And personally, Doctor Braddock, I felt heaps better in my own mind when I knew he was doing the job."

"And I, too. Why, he knows the lad! He's been watching his case for months—he and Martin. Mrs. Fisher's just plain dumb!"

"And again—so say we all!" Ellen said emphatically. She went on into the hall. On the bulletin board was a notice that she was to report at seven in the morning to room sixty-seven. That was the room where the beautiful Mrs. Hartley was convalescing from influenza combined with a slightly congested gall bladder. Good! She suddenly felt relaxed and happy again.

Terry Morley telephoned to invite her to the pictures and dinner.

"Grand, Terry! I feel just like a binge," she told him.

A warm soothing bath and bed! How good to stretch out and feel the exquisite waves of drowsiness envelope one's tired body and weary mind!

Marcella Harris burst into Ellen's room soon after two that afternoon to tell her that Tony Fisher's toes itched! He was in a cast for a few weeks but for the first time in six years his toes itched! Marcella shouted with laughter.

"Isn't that the craziest thing you ever heard? His mother ran out to tell me as I passed the door just now. The woman was so excited that she didn't even see me. I'm sure she never would have spoken if she had. I asked Braddock about it and he said it was probably all her imagination or Tony's, that it was far too soon to tell. Anyway, he is partly conscious and everything is running smooth as silk."

"Thanks, Marcy," Ellen murmured, yawning widely and snuggling deeper into her blankets, "but please get out. I'm not getting up until dinner. I've got a heavy date tonight—worse luck!"

"Okay," Marcella laughed, quite unoffended. "But think of all you're missing. The place is swarming with visiting bigwigs and littlewigs. Too bad Murdock isn't here. She'd make short work of some of them. Better change your mind and come down, Ellen. Cy Dent is acting cicerone to the Corinth nurses—one is a dizzy blonde."

"Who cares?" muttered Ellen, sleepily. "Only get out and in passing you might hang a sign on my door—'Do Not Disturb'!"

And that's just what Marcella Harris did and that's why Ellen slept through dinner and on until six the next morning when Marcella stopped on her way to her room for a letter she had forgotten to mail. She took down the sign and went in, not too quietly. The girl was sleeping soundly and Marcella stood for a moment looking down at her. How lovely she was, and such a peach! The older nurse laid a gentle hand on her forehead and Ellen opened wide brown eyes, still cloudy with dreams.

"Well, my girl, you did sleep! Know what time it is?"

Ellen sat up, stretched her arms high about her head.

"W-what time is it?" she yawned.

"Six o'clock—six a.m., my dear."

"Wh-at?" Ellen's eyes were open now, her gaze incredulous. "Really, Marcy? Did I sleep all that time? And I meant to see that picture at the Royal. Terry Morley—"

"Oh, he called and Josephine told him there was a sign on your door that you were not to be disturbed. That probably the doctor put it there and there's a basket of roses with his card on it in the bathroom. I'll bring it in while you collect your wits."

Ellen reached for her mules and a robe and was still stretching and yawning when Marcella returned.

"Take it up to L, Marcy," Ellen said, as she read Terry's message; regret for her indisposition. "I'm working for the idle rich during the next few days and probably will be smothered in flowers. They're lovely, though, aren't they? He's a peach, Marcy!"

"So?" Marcella took the flowers and left. Ellen grinned to herself. She could almost see the thoughts that streamed in one long colorful parade through Marcella's romantic brain.

CHAPTER SEVENTEEN

MRS. HARTLEY WAS young and beautiful. Ellen remembered that she was a Brentwood girl who two years before had
married some man from St. Louis and had gone there to
live. She remembered it had been a brilliant affair—one the
town talked of for days before and after the event.

Flowers filled every available space in the room and
more arrived hourly. Ellen wondered why she didn't send
some of them to the wards and made up her mind she
would suggest it when they were better acquainted.

"Doctor MacGowan told me I was to have a new nurse.
Are you Miss Gaylord?" Mrs. Hartley asked as Ellen began her morning ministrations.

"Yes, Mrs. Hartley. I'm Ellen Gaylord, very much at
your service."

"I'm so glad you're pretty," the other said frankly. "I'm
sick of looking at plain girls. What a lot of them you
have here!"

"I hadn't noticed," Ellen answered. "They are all so
wonderful!"

"Are they?" Mrs. Hartley spoke indifferently. "When
flowers or fruit arrive, please give me the cards. You may
pass on the fruit to anyone you wish—I can't eat it. I enjoy
flowers, though."

"What a lot you have!" Ellen exclaimed as she picked
up a huge vase of American Beauties. "I'll just change the
water in them—"

"Don't bother. There will be dozens more. If they're wilt-
ed, throw them out. And those carnations—throw them out,
too. Carnations! He would send carnations—they last long-
est. Dad's a thrifty soul, poor lamb!"

Ellen made a promise to herself that the carnations
should go up to Pediatrics—children always liked carnations—they stood a lot of handling. She dutifully removed
the offending floral offerings and put fresh water in the
vases of those still in favor. During the morning more
flowers arrived and Ellen saw that her patient's peevishness
increased with the reading of each succeeding card.

Doctor Dent dropped in about ten o'clock and he and
Mrs. Hartley met like old friends. To Ellen he was professional and impersonal—even a little stiff. Mrs. Hartley

teased him about some mutual friend—a Gladys Mason, who was about due to arrive any minute. Ellen thought Doctor Dent lingered a bit longer than was necessary; but at last he departed with scarcely a glance in her direction.

Mrs. Hartley eyed Ellen, her glance speculative. At last she asked with disarming candor.

"Is it you Cy Dent is crazy over? Oh, don't mind me," at Ellen's start and flush of annoyance. "I'm brutally frank —always was. I heard he was enamored of some girl in Anthony Ware and you're the only one I've seen so far he'd look at twice."

"Well," Ellen answered coldly, "I assure you it isn't I."

"Why, don't you like him—Ellen, isn't it? You might just as well tell me, for I shall find out sooner or later. I always do."

"I didn't say I disliked him, Mrs. Hartley. Perhaps— shall we say it's just that I'm not interested in men?" Ellen was furious. What right had this girl to catechise her.

"How unnatural and how perfectly absurd! You remind me of an ostrich—Oh, for heaven's sake, don't get peev- ed!" as Ellen stiffened. "It's your own affair, of course, but I still think you're putting on an act. Maybe you'll land a bigger fish because of it—men are a queer lot. I thought I knew all there was to know about them when I married Sam Hartley, but—" Her voice grew suddenly husky and Ellen looked at her in surprise—"he fooled me."

Ellen hoped she wasn't going to make a confidant of her; but apparently, she had said all she intended saying then, for she turned over and was so quiet that Ellen thought she slept.

Gladys Mason arrived some time later.

"Don't go, Ellen," Mrs. Hartley said. "This is my new nurse, Glad—Ellen Gaylord—Gladys Mason, my best friend and worst enemy. I like having you about, Ellen—you're decorative, isn't she, Glad? And let me tell you something, I won't give two cents for your chances with Doc—not while she's unshackled."

Ellen tried not to listen. Her cheeks burned with anger and humiliation. She busied herself with a fresh box of flowers and over and over to herself she repeated a for- mula from her adolescent days, when, shy and deeply emotional, she had been susceptible to the spitefulness and jealousy of her plainer schoolmates.

"She can't hurt me—no one can hurt me—I refuse to be hurt!"

Gradually, her anger faded and she turned her usual, lovely, serene face toward them, but they had already forgotten her existence.

Ellen thought Gladys Mason the most fascinating girl she had ever seen. Small, dark and vivacious, she flitted about the flower-filled room, examining each vase and basket, asking the name of the donor and relating something amusing about each one.

"Nothing from Sam, I see—yet, or is it too precious for display? I tell you, Jan, the boy's mad with jealousy. Why don't you make the first move?"

Ellen thought. "They talk and act as if I were deaf and blind. They'll be telling their most intimate secrets first thing they know. Oh, this is a grand life—this job of nursing, especially to the idle rich."

And that is just what happened. Within the short space of time Gladys Mason spent with her patient, Ellen learned that Sam Hartley had walked out on his wife and that she had come home forthwith and had started suit for divorce. She learned the cause, too. A certain Roland Emsden of polo fame had been spending rather a lot of time at the Hartley mansion, in fact, rumor had it that he was the man in the case.

"As if I would look twice at Rolly Emsden," scoffed Janet Hartley.

Gladys laughed. "But darling, you did look at him and many more times than twice."

"Well, and what if I did!" the other demanded. "Was I to let Sam dictate to me where and how and with whom I spent my time? He's gone all day—presumably on business. How do I know it's always business? He may be having affairs with a dozen women; but do I act like an idiot about it? I ask you."

Gladys shrugged and Ellen felt like telling her patient that she certainly did act like an idiot. The injured lady went on with her grievance.

"Sam was positively abusive—insulting. He's so old fashioned, Glad. Sometime I wonder why I ever married him."

"So do I," Miss Mason murmured and smiled disarmingly at the sudden offence in the other's face. "Why did you?" she asked.

"You ask me that?" Mrs. Hartley demanded. "Why, you know very well that we were simply mad about each other —before we were married. Sometimes I wonder if that feeling ever lasts, Glad."

"It doesn't," the other said flatly.

"How do you know, you've never—"

"Just the same, I know. In marriages that stick—it's replaced by something better, or at least something saner."

Mrs. Hartley moved restlessly. "But who wants a safe and sane life?"

Gladys shook her head at her and said nothing for a moment. Then she changed the subject entirely to people they both knew and places they both had visited.

Ellen thought that for all her inconsequential light chatter, Gladys Mason was much more of a woman than the supposedly poised and sophisticated Mrs. Hartley.

On the way down to lunch, Doctor Dent intercepted Ellen in the corridor.

"Don't let Jan Hartley get under your skin, Nightingale," he warned. "She's a spoiled brat as the result of too much sparing the rod. I hope Sam holds out on her."

"You would! How you men stick together! Probably she is well rid of him if only she could be made to see it, for he certainly can't care a great deal for her." Ellen didn't know why she suddenly veered to the side of Mrs. Hartley when all along her sympathy had been with the husband.

"Why? Because he won't let her continue to make a monkey out of him?"

"I doubt if she was responsible for that," Ellen said coolly and attempted to pass him but he barred the way. His hand brushed lightly across her shoulder.

"Still carrying that chip, I see. Tell me, Nightingale, what has the charming Terry got that the rest of us males lack?"

"I wear no chip on my shoulder, Doctor Dent," Ellen said stiffly, "and you can't possibly be interested in my friends. Please let me pass."

For a moment Ellen thought he was going to shake her. His blue eyes darkened and flashed dangerously. His hands reached for her, then dropped to his side. He shrugged as if in futility, turned abruptly and strode away. And if he heard Ellen's quick and penitent:

"Oh, Cy, I'm sorry!" he gave no sign.

CHAPTER EIGHTEEN

"YOU'VE BEEN SUCH a grand pal, Ellen, that I'm going to tell you a secret." Terry Morley and Ellen were resting between dances at the Cosmopolitan in Corinth one night in late March. The air was mild and Ellen felt excited and eager as the approach of spring always made her. And she had on a new gown—a hyacinth blue crepe with a long, very full skirt, snug fitting bodice, tiny puffed sleeves and practically no back. It made her feel young and gay and sophisticated.

"I'm sure it's a nice secret, Terry," she laughed—"because your eyes sparkle and you seem just about ready to burst. So perhaps you'd better hurry before something really embarrassing happens."

"Vi is going to marry me after all." He spoke with a sort of ecstatic awe.

"Vi? But—but—I thought she—oh, Terry, I think that's grand!" Ellen wondered why the news should cause her such sudden lightness of heart. After all, they were neither of them especially intimate friends. She knew Terry much the better and liked him far more than she did Lady Violet. But what about Cy? Where did he come into the picture? She thought it well not to ask.

"Oh, I know what you meant to say, Ellen," Terry said without hestitation. "She had a fool idea that she owed her life to Dent, therefore he had a right to it. Just a crazy romantic notion girls get sometimes. When I told her that she had had a double dose of your blood and therefore owed you twice as much as she owed Dent, she saw the light. She sent word to you that she feared she had perhaps lacked appreciation of your kindness. I told her that she had sort of passed you up and I, for one, couldn't understand why. It was then that she told me she hoped I hadn't changed toward her for she had discovered it was me—I, after all. That's the whole story."

"I'm glad, Terry. She's very lovely and I think you're quite nice, yourself."

"Thank you kindly, lady. Since I hurt my knee, I can't do some of the things I used to and so perhaps squiring won't be so bad, after all. I'm not so keen about spending my life over there, but no doubt we'll be back and forth a lot. One thing I hope is that you'll come over and see us some time."

Ellen laughed, happiness bubbling up in her heart. Spring was such a wonderful season! No matter how tired one was and how dark things had looked—spring just sort of rejuvenated one—lifted one's spirits so that the world became another place entirely. What would life be without its recurring springs? Oh, it was grand to be alive and young and—and not too hard on the eyes. To be wearing a brand new and extremely becoming frock. To be sitting across from an attractive young man—who was engaged to another girl! Yes, that last was perhaps the grandest of all.

"I doubt if I shall ever have money enough to do much ocean travelling, Terry. Nurses can't accumulate a great deal, you know, and every cent I do manage to save is going into a fund to help me through medical school."

Terry shook his head positively. "Never. You'll never get that far, gorgeous. If Vi hadn't possessed every inch of my heart, your nursing days would end right here and now."

"Oh, Terry, that doesn't make any hit with me," Ellen said calmly. "I hear so much of that sort of tommy-rot! Like all males you take it for granted that you have only to beckon and I'll follow."

"Beckon nothing," Terry retorted sharply. "I'd pick you up and set you down hard in some place where you would have to learn to love me, willy-nilly. I know women, beautiful."

"Hmm. Cave-man stuff," scoffed Ellen.

"Sure. You're the type that needs that sort of treatment. Sometimes I think I'll put—no matter—skip it. Mind your own business, is my watchword. Come on, let's dance. I'm glad I told you about Vi and me."

"And so am I, Terry, and I wish you both all the luck and happiness in the world!"

Ellen thought she never had spent a more enjoyable evening, and when Terry and she got out at the Nurses' Home just after midnight, she was surprised to see Doctor Dent coming from the steps. Now, what was he doing here? Which of the girls was he rushing now? They passed with a simple cool "good evening." Terry unlocked the door, pressed her hand with a soft: "good-night" and Ellen went quickly up the stairs to her room. The house was very quiet. Whoever Doctor Dent had been calling on must have made a rapid retreat for there wasn't a sound as she closed her door. Of course it might have been Mrs. Drake he had come to see—she had been having trouble with a lame shoulder for the past day or two. If it was one of the girls, he was certainly a lightning change artist. "Off with the old love and on with the new" in record time. What a man!

She wondered just what, if anything, had happened between Lady Violet Terrill and him. He had intimated only the other day that he still heard from her. She had cared for him, Ellen was sure. Oh, well, what did it matter, anyway? He was nothing in her young life. But just the same, she was glad he wasn't going to marry her—Maybe this Gladys Mason was the real one. Mrs. Hartley had teased him about her. But what was he doing at the Home? He must have been calling on one of the girls or perhaps had just brought her back from some place. Still, he had no car with him. No, he must just have been making a call. Now, which one of the girls had he shown particular admiration for? She couldn't tell. That they all adored him she knew; but which one was the fortunate—favorite, she corrected quickly.

She got into bed and expected to fall asleep immediately. But that question kept recurring and played havoc with her dreams. She tossed and turned and at last got up and walked about the room on her toes; stood before the open window and breathed deeply of the clear, cold spring air, then determinedly got into bed again and composed herself for slumber; but the first faint gray of morning marked her windows before she fell into an exhausted sleep from which Marcella Harris wakened her, it seemed but a moment later. However, a quick shower did wonders for her and she was ready with the others to go down to breakfast.

Mrs. Hartley was in an irritable mood again this morning. She was sleeping badly and Ellen knew she was not convalescing as she should. Sam Hartley persisted in his complete silence and Ellen felt she would like to take them both and knock their heads together in the hope that a little sense might be jarred loose. And even if it was none of her business, she was glad she had taken a hand in the straightening out of their foolish difficulty. "Mind your own business" was Terry Morley's motto and it was a good one for everyone to follow ordinarily, but just the same—

The lady wanted no breakfast although Ellen had prepared an especially attractive tray. The room was stuffy and when the windows were opened, she complained of freezing to death. She wanted to see no one this morning—they all bored her to tears. When Doctor MacGowan stopped in on his round, she snubbed him unmercifully so that he was more dour and more Scotch than ever. Ellen was at her wit's end when the first box of flowers arrived. The patient brightened for a moment and reached for them, read the accompanying card and threw box and flowers across the room. Then she turned over on her face and wept.

Ellen picked up the flowers and put them in water. Poor girl! Ellen knew what the matter was and wished she had the courage to tell Janet Hartley to brace up—everything was going to be fine. But of course, that was entirely outside her province. She was a nurse not a mender of broken marriages and while she might take it upon herself, in a way, to occasionally assist. Providence, it was a risky business and not to be made a practice of. She wished people had more sense—especially people in love. It was a great nuisance!

Doctor Dent came in at eleven and attempted his usual pleasantry only to be snapped at and told to get out. He stared quizzically at the back of the dark head buried in the pillow then turned to Ellen.

"We'll have a 'No Visitors' sign on the door tomorrow, Gaylord. I agree with Mac—too many callers." He raised one eyebrow as Mrs. Hartley flounced over on the bed.

"Don't you dare!" she stormed, and Ellen saw that her face was streaked with tears. "I'll go mad if I'm left alone here!"

"You won't be alone. Your nurse will be right here within call. Now be a good girl and relax and rest. You'll be out of this place before you know it if you will only co-operate a bit."

"Co-operate a bit!" she mimicked. "Why should I co-operate? No one ever has co-operated with me. Oh, I—

I'm so unhappy!" Down went the head once more and the slight frame shook with sobs.

"Here, here, this will never do," Doctor Dent said, and Ellen resented what she thought was his impatience. "Come on, Jan," he wheedled, "tell me all about it. Maybe I can help. Or maybe you'd rather tell Gaylord—she will understand, I'm sure. She's the understandingest female on the staff." He grinned at Ellen and patted the weeping girl.

"It's S-Sam," she whimpered. "He—he hasn't been near me and he hasn't even—not one flower! O-oh, I—I—hate him for hurting me s-so! Why doesn't he come?"

Cy stared wide-eyed at Ellen who couldn't repress a smile at Janet Hartley's inconsistency. "Oh, is that all?" he asked her as she burrowed deeper into her pillow. "I thought you and Sam, (or was it just you?) had come to the parting of the ways—decided to call it a day. Isn't that why you came home to mother, Jan?"

"Shut up, you—you—! Oh, why did he ever let me go? I'm his wife and he ought to have prevented me from leaving him!"

"For heaven's sake, Jan, be your age and generation! This is Nineteen-thirty-eight, woman! Husbands don't use the iron hand any more—I doubt if men have any iron in their systems the way you women wind us 'round your fingers. Sam probably thought you were fed up and rarin' to get out and so, wanting you to keep happy, he let you go."

"But I'm not happy, Cy. I—I'm mis-er-able!"

"Gosh, girl, don't begin that again! Quit weeping. Sam'll probably be tickled pink to know you haven't quit. Why not tell him so?"

"Tell him? You mean he is—"

"No. He isn't just outside. That only happens in the movies. He's probably still in St. Louis, if he hasn't gone to South America as he talked of doing," he said brutally. "There—there! Lord, Ellen, do something! She's started again!" He got to his feet and bolted for the door. Ellen had a hard time to keep from laughing aloud. It was all so childish and ridiculous! He opened the door the barest crack to whisper: "Call MacGowan if she doesn't quit. Give her a bromide. I'm no good at this sort of thing."

"I'll say you're not," Ellen murmured and grinned at him as he withdrew.

Mrs. Hartley had stopped crying. She mopped her eyes with a sodden handkerchief. Ellen bathed the flushed, tear-stained face very gently.

"My head aches frightfully," the patient moaned.

"I'll bring you an ice pack and fix you something quieting, and then you can have a little nap. Things are bound to improve, soon. You'll see."

"You're sweet," Mrs. Hartley murmured.

The room grew very quiet. Ellen received boxes of flowers and took care of them without disturbing the patient. But she saw that none of them came from Sam Hartley. Suppose he should prove to be one of the stubborn sort. Suppose he didn't want to "continue being a monkey" for his wife's amusement. Oh, but he must come!

It was nearly five o'clock when Cy Dent poked his head in at the door and beckoned Ellen. "Sam is downstairs," he whispered. "How is she?"

"Sleeping. Have him come up. I'll slip out as soon as he gets here."

Sam Hartley was a big, red-haired, boyish young fellow, with eyes like a spaniel and a hesitant way of speaking. Ellen smiled at him and motioned him to enter. She closed the door softly and sat down in the corridor nearby. Cy Dent came to her there.

"So you wired him, too, did you, Nightingale?" he said, his eyes quizzical.

"Too? Then you—"

" 'Two minds with but a single thought,
    Two hearts—'
who was it, said that?"

"I haven't the least idea. Someone terribly sentimental," Ellen answered. "But I do hope they patch up their differences. I think it's too bad when two people marry that they can't pull together and be willing to give and take."

"Ain't it the truth?" Cy agreed. "What's that—Lord! I never knew it to fail," as the eerie hollow sound of a loud speaker broke into what he hoped might be a friendly chat. "Doctor Dent—Emergency—calling Doctor Dent—Emergency—calling Doctor Dent—"

146

Ellen watched him hurry down the corridor and take the stairs four at a time. She smiled to herself. It was queer that they both had had the same idea. Of course she had no business butting into the Hartleys' private affairs; but just the same, Mrs. Hartley was making herself ill over their quarrel and just one look at Sam Hartley told Ellen she had made no mistake. Just two silly, spoiled children who had not yet found the real meaning of life. Ellen felt very mature and wise.

It was some time before she received a summons to return to her patient and what a change she found! Mrs. Hartley was sitting up in bed, her hands held tightly in those of her husband who wore a fatuous and slightly shamefaced grin as she introduced him to Ellen.

"I'm glad I'm going home soon, Sam," she said after a moment when she watched her husband with adoring eyes. "Ellen's so pretty that it might be too much of a temptation if you saw her every day. And darling, she thinks she doesn't care for men—isn't that a scream? Sort of a nasty blow to your vanity, eh what? Of course, I don't believe her—not with her face. And listen, darling, I think Cy Dent—well—doesn't exactly hate her." She laughed gleefully. "See her blush, Sam? Isn't she delicious?"

"Oh, have a heart, Jan! You're not being fair—quite rude, in fact. After all, m'dear, personalities aren't exactly good form, you know. Miss Gaylord has a perfect right to her inhibitions, an' all that."

Ellen wondered if he were English and decided he must be. An Englishman from St. Louis! Later she found that he had had a year at Oxford—only a year, and it had done that to him! She wished she could watch Cy while he listened to him talk. Cy had such a keen sense of humor and suddenly she felt herself blushing, and refused to acknowledge to herself that it was because she was feeling kindly toward him.

CHAPTER NINETEEN

APRIL BROUGHT SHEETS of rain and boisterous winds. The hospital had calmed down after its hectic bout with influenza, and Ellen looked forward longingly to her week's rest. At last it seemed likely she would get it. But she didn't write Aunt Bess until the last minute. She had disappointed her twice already this spring.

"So you're off for a whole week? Grand! And you certainly need it," Marcella Harris said as she stopped in at Ellen's room after Chapel one Sunday morning. "Cy Dent's off, too. Left this morning, I believe. Cy looks sort of worried lately. Noticed it? Maybe that Boston job isn't panning out quite to his satisfaction. Heard anything?"

Ellen's thoughts raced. Cy hadn't mentioned going away when he waylaid her in the lower hall last night. Oh, well, it was his own business and none of hers. But it was queer, for he knew she was having a week—he had congratulated her on getting it and hoped she would have a good rest. His shoulder seemed to be all right now, and he had been working double duty ever since Doctor Braddock had fallen ill. He had asked again about Terry Morley and she had been tempted to tell him about his engagement to Violet but decided not to. Let him find it out for himself. And then he had said:

"So your wonderful Terry Morley is to become an expatriate."

"Oh, how do you know?" Ellen asked.

"I saw him over at the Club a couple of days ago and he told me. Fine chap, Morley."

"Exceptionally so, I think," Ellen agreed. "Lady X is to be congratulated."

"Ah, but one doesn't congratulate the bride, Nightingale," he teased.

"Just the same, I think she's to be congratulated," Ellen insisted, stubbornly. "Terry's a darling—I like him a lot."

"So I understand," Cy said without enthusiasm. "He said the same about you. Too bad—"

"Don't say it, Doctor Dent. You ought to know by this time that I am not interested in men," Ellen reminded him.

"No? Well, as it happens, I had no intention of saying what you think I did. What a one you are to jump at conclusions! I intended saying: Too bad I couldn't say the same about Lady X. There! See? You were miles off."

Ellen's smile was skeptical. Her look said plainly she didn't believe him. She started on.

"Well, good-bye, Nightingale. Have a good rest and please do something about that disposition—it's really growing worse. Sad, in one so young and so lovely!" He grinned after her, then shook his head.

Ellen's back had stiffened and she held her head high as she mounted the stairs to the Male Surgical where she was putting in her last night before her vacation. Well, thank goodness she wouldn't have to encounter him for a whole week! What bliss! Disposition, indeed! What business was it of his, anyway? And she would give him to understand that there was not one thing wrong with her disposition— not one thing. The trouble was with his perverted sense of humor. She sighed, for she had to acknowledge that Cy Dent had the power to rouse every bit of temper and perversity she possessed. She hated to acknowledge it even to herself. But it was true and what enjoyment he could possibly get from ragging her, puzzled her.

Now she answered Marcella carelessly: "Not a thing. Oh, he'll get that job all right with Doctor MacGowan's backing."

"Perhaps that's where he's gone now," Marcella offered, her eyes inquisitive.

"Perhaps." Ellen's tone was quite indifferent and she yawned as she prepared for her warm bath. Marcella lingered for a moment, her face puzzled. Something was going on that she couldn't fathom. Still, she had discovered it was not wise to persist on the subject of Cy Dent with Ellen, and reluctantly took her departure.

Ellen lay down for a while after her bath. She would leave on the ten o'clock bus. She would have to change to a jitney ten miles from Deacon's Landing, but she didn't mind. She would reach Aunt Bess' soon after two, in ample time for dinner. She didn't mind the rain, either—rather liked it, in fact—sort of matched her mood. Disposition, indeed! Just what did he mean by doing something about her disposition? She would have Cy Dent know that her disposition was considered exceptional. She determinedly put him out of her mind and tried to sleep. After tossing about for half an hour she got up and packed her suitcase. Then decided she might as well wash her hair and give herself a manicure. She just couldn't sleep. Reaction from so much night work, of course. She called a taxi and went back to her room to put on her coat. Josephine picked up her suitcase and carried it downstairs to the front porch.

"A turrible day, Miss Gaylord," the maid said as she held open the hall door for her. "I never saw it rain any harder. Hope you don't run into any floods or fogs either —they's plenty of 'em up no'th."

"Not in my part of the state, Josephine," Ellen reassured her. "Good-bye, be a good girl while I'm gone."

Ellen always gave that parting bit of advice when she left and Josephine found it very comical. Now she grinned toothily, her black eyes sparkling with amusement. "I'll try, Miss Gaylord, and you be one, too."

The driver of the taxi stood at the foot of the steps waiting with an open umbrella. The rain splashed on his shining puttees and long gray slicker. He shut Ellen into the big car and she thought vaguely that the taxi company must have some new automobiles. This one was positively luxurious. She wished she could afford to have it take her the whole way to Deacon's Landing—she would have a nap, then. She watched the rain run in little dancing rivers down Main Street hill. The sky was a gray curtain, the trees with their young green leaves looked drowned, the hills beyond were a misty blur, and people hurrying along, to and from Church, were giant mushrooms of varying colors. She closed her eyes for a moment. How delicious to glide smoothly and quietly like this! She must be nearly at the Terminal. She sat up abruptly. They had passed Market Street where the Bus Terminal was. She rapped sharply on the glass. The driver lowered the window without turning his head.

"I told you the Bus Terminal," she reminded him, hoping she had not missed that ten o'clock bus.

"I have orders to drive you to Deacon's Landing, Miss," the driver said civilly. Ellen sank back. Doctor MacGowan, of course. He knew how very tired she was and knew of that change to the jitney ten miles from her destination. How very thoughtful of him! She wished she could rid herself of the feeling that some day she would have to hurt him. How had she ever gotten the idea that he was particularly interested in her? Ann, of course. He had been grand to her and it did seem to her that he liked her. Oh, dear! Life was so complicated at times! Dear Doctor MacGowan how could she hurt him? But maybe it was only a fatherly interest. She smiled dubiously. He wasn't old enough for that. She wondered if Doctor Dent had really gone to Boston. She had heard that his home was somewhere in this state.

They reached open country. How dreary it all looked! A man sloshed to a barn through rivers of mud. Cows huddled together in a barnyard, their hides sleek with wet. Bedraggled chickens pecked half-heartedly and optimistically shook themselves from time to time. Only the ducks seemed to enjoy the day as they waddled along in the mire, stopping occasionaly to scoop into a particularly murky puddle. A gray, depressing day—a day to fit her mood!

She looked at her watch. Eleven o'clock. About a third of the way there. Drowsiness overcame her and she slept. Her dreams were fantastic. In them Doctor Dent sang a lullaby as he gently rocked her to sleep.

"Sleep, dear Nightingale, sleep as we sail,
      Sleep, sleep, s-l-e-e-p-p-p—"

"Stop it!" she said aloud, and awoke. She looked around with puzzled eyes. Oh, yes. She was on her way to Deacon's Landing to stay with Aunt Bess. Doctor MacGowan had arranged for her to be driven the whole way. Good, kind, Doctor MacGowan!

The man in front had removed his cap. Ellen was startled at the resemblance to Cy Dent. Blond head, broad shoulders —she raised her eyes and encountered quizzical blue ones in the little mirror. She gasped and cried aloud:

"You? What—how—"

The car stopped. He turned to grin at her.

"Hello, Nightingale! Have a pleasant forty winks? I hoped you would sleep the entire two hundred miles. I was held up back there by a long freight—that's probably what wakened you."

"But—but—" she stammered in bewilderment.

"Why not come up front so we can talk easily?" he invited.

"Just tell me—just explain—"

"Okay. So you refuse my invitation? Very well. I'm on my way home—it's only about fifty miles from your stop—south. I knew you were planning on going to your aunt's and knew also that if I offered you a lift you would shrivel me, and as I thoroughly dislike riding alone, especially on a day like this, I worked out this grand little scheme."

"But this isn't your car."

"Of course it isn't. It belongs to Sam Hartley. If you had taken the time to notice, you'd have seen it bears Missouri license plates. It's mine for a week, however. Sam's a good scout in spite of his Oxford accent and his taste in wives. Isn't this better than a bus, Nightingale? Tell the truth, now."

"Of course it's far more comfortable," Ellen acknowledged; "but I wish you hadn't bothered."

"No bother at all, lady. It's a pleasure, only, I'm afraid I'm going to get a crick in my neck—"

"Oh, close the window and drive on. I'm not in the mood for conversation." Ellen spoke crossly. Why did he always put her in embarrassing situations? If Miss Forsyth or Doctor MacGowan knew of this there would be a lot of explaining to do. Darn him! Why couldn't he mind his own business? Well, it wasn't necessary to slam that window. It's a wonder it didn't break. Cy was mad, she could tell from the set of his chin. Well, she didn't care. She hadn't asked him to do this. It was another of his brilliant ideas.

The car gathered speed. The wet countryside was now a long gray smear. Up hill and down, through village and hamlet, past dense dripping woods and misty, pale green meadows. A smile touched the corners of Ellen's mouth. Cy was like that. Rouse him and he did things. She rapped on the glass as they neared Deacon's Landing. Without turning his head, he again lowered the window between them.

"Turn to your right at this next corner, and if you want to deliver me in one unbroken piece, you'd better drive a little slower. This road isn't any too good along here after heavy rains."

Up went the window with a bang. Ellen giggled. He stopped the car so suddenly that she slid forward to the edge of the seat and her new spring hat shifted to a position over one ear.

"So you find the situation amusing, do you?" he shouted through the glass. "For two cents I'd take you across my knee and give you a demonstration that would be even more amusing—to me."

Ellen gasped again, her brown eyes enormous in her tired face. "You wouldn't dare!" she shrieked.

"Better not dare me, Nightingale," he warned. "I've stood just about all your whimsies I'm going to. Do you hear? You've badgered, abused, teased and irritated me almost beyond endurance. You're gloried in snubbing me: You've made my life miserable. You've—you've—"

"I? I've done all that? You're crazy! It's you—you—, Cy Dent, who have kept me on thorns these months and months! You've pestered the life out of me. You've hounded me and harassed me and all the time just—just amused yourself at my expense. You've—you've made my life miserable just to indulge your perverted sense of humor. It's useless to deny it. You—you know it's true. What are you going to do?" she gasped as he slid out from beneath the wheel and swung open the door beside her.

"Do? What do you suppose I'm going to do? I'm going to get this thing straightened out once and for all time. I'm sick and tired of having you make a complete monkey out of me. Now you listen to me, Ellen Gaylord. You have known for months that I'm crazy in love with you—"

"What?" Ellen whispered. "You're what?"

"In love — love — love! Don't you know what that means?" he asked as she stared at him in unbelief. He lurched forward, slipped an arm about her shoulders and pulled her close. "I'll show you what I mean, you little idiot —you little icicle—you little witch!" His lips clung to hers for a long moment. Her head fell back against his shoulder and her brown eyes searched his. A wave of color chased the tiredness from her face and she stammered after a moment when her eyes fell from the look of adoration in his blue ones.

"Why—you do, don't you?"

He laughed joyously and drew her to him again.

"I'll tell the world! And—now you say it, Nightingale. You do, don't you?"

"Do what?" she asked dreamily. So this is what had ailed her! Ann had been right all the time. What a little sap she was! How was it possible for a girl to reach the age of twenty-one and not recognize love when it came to her? Women were supposed to be so clever that way, far cleverer than mere males. So it had been love that had made her edgy and short tempered and moody, she mused, while Cy searched her face with loving yet anxious eyes. His arms tightened about her and he bent his face again to hers.

"Tell me, darling. You do love me, don't you? Not as much as I love you, of course—you couldn't, but enough to marry me?"

Ellen sat up. She drew back from his encircling arms. "But—but I intended being a doctor, Cy. I told Mac that, and he was all for it."

"I know and Mac told you that being a doctor's wife wasn't so bad—that a man could go far if he had a lass like you at hame keeping his hearthstone warm."

"How did you know?"

"Oh, Uncle Mac told me. He's been plugging for me all year—in fact, before that. He's been worried I'd follow in his footsteps and pick the wrong girl, sweetheart. He's all for this match, Nightingale. If you don't marry me I—I've a notion he'll disown me."

"Uncle? Is Doctor MacGowan really your uncle?"

"Sure. My mother's younger brother. We've kept it dark of course. Ethics—rot! It wouldn't have been just the thing for me to interne at Anthony Ware if it were known—not while Uncle Mac was Chief of Staff. The old boy's such a stickler for form. But I held out for it and I'm glad."

Ellen experienced a let-down feeling and yet it was one of relief, too. So she wouldn't have to hurt Angus Mac-Gowan, after all. Ann again. How silly she had been. As if a man like Doctor MacGowan could ever stoop to a chit like her! She blushed and Cy kissed her again, then drew back.

"How stubborn you are! Do you or don't you love me, Ellen Gaylord?" Cy's arms were close to his sides now. His voice was no longer fond but clear and crisp.

"Why, of course I do. You've told me a dozen times that I did, haven't you? But—"

"We have all our lives to ask and answer questions, darling. Just now I'm going to make up for all the times you've held me off when I've wanted to take you in my arms."

The rain fell in sheets and the trees dripped soddenly, but the two were quite oblivious. Inside the car it was dry and warm, and there was so much to talk about! Ellen was the first to realize the passing of time.

"Aunt Bess will be frantic and imagine all sorts of things have happened, Cy. We must go right on this minute. Why can't you stay on a few days at Deacon's Landing? Aunt Bess can put you up."

"I was going to ask you to come home with me. Mother will want to meet you—she ought to know you already, I've talked enough about you. Why not do that? Explain it to Aunt Bess, she'll understand. I want you to meet Doc, too. And we might look for a house while we're about it. There'll be no delay, Nightingale. Understand that."

"A house, Cy in Wyckham? But I thought—you said— what about—"

"Boston?" he laughed. "I never had any intention of accepting that Boston job, in fact it's already filled. No, darling, you're going to be the wife of a general practitioner. Are you terribly disappointed?"

Ellen gave him a little push.

"Hypothetical case!" she jeered, then drew his head down to hers. "I'd have gone to Boston with you, of course, but deep down in my heart I should have been unhappy. I think I've always wanted to be a doctor's wife. A real, honest-to-goodness, heart-and-soul-as-well-as-head doctor, like—"

"Uncle John, I know," said Cy.

"What a lot you know about me!" Ellen demurred. "And I—

"Don't worry, sweetheart, you'll soon know all the horrible truth about me—after you've met mother and Doc. What the one doesn't tell the other will; but they're grand people! You'll adore them."

CHAPTER TWENTY

GRADUATION! ELLEN AWOKE to a perfect June day. A day of brilliant sunshine, soft perfume-laden breezes, and a general air of excitement. Early though it was, the house was awake and she could hear the flip-flopping of slippered feet in the halls as the girls passed to and from the bathrooms and showers. One or two rapped softly on her door and Ann Murdock thrust in her head to inquire if she intended getting up at all that morning.

But Ellen was loath to get up. She lay and dreamed of all the things—delightful and rather frightening—some that had already come to pass and others that were to happen within the next few weeks. Tonight after the exercises, she was to announce her engagement to Cyrus Dent. She wondered if it would come as a surprise to the girls. She had told no one, not even Ann—or, as she said to herself, especially Ann. She was afraid of hurting her. But she intended telling her first of all—just before they should go down to the chapel where the exercises were to be held..

Poor Ann! And yet Ellen felt sure that Ann would find her happiness some day. There was something appealing and very endearing about her. None of the smart sophistication, the hard, biting brilliance that so often hurt and antagonized people.

"For heaven's sake, get up, girl!" Marcella Harris came into the room, her arms piled high with clean linen. "Here, I sorted out your laundry for you. What ails you—not sick?"

Ellen laughed joyously. "Sick? Who, me? Just lazy, I guess, Marcy, and I hate to leave the bed I've occupied more or less regularly for three years. Perhaps I shall sleep here tonight, but I may not. Aunt Bess is coming to commencement and wants me to go back with her. She's driving."

"Does that mean we won't see you again after today, Ellen?" Marcella asked, her eyes clouded. "I'm going to miss you—terribly."

"I'll miss you, too, Marcy. I'll miss the whole place, when I have time to think about it. But you see, I'm expecting to be very busy so perhaps I won't have so much time to think —about myself and the hospital, I mean."

At the forlorn look in the plain face of the older nurse, Ellen said, impulsively: "If you only knew how much I appreciate all you've done for me, Marcy, you'd realize I'll miss you all the rest of my life!"

There was a rush of footsteps and three or four girls burst into the room. "Do you know what time it is? Quarter of seven! You'll never make it, Gaylord. And this is our last breakfast together, too. Do get up and come down with us."

Ann shouldered herself past the others. "What's the idea, Ellen? Sick?"

"Get out—all of you!" Ellen laughed. "I'll be ready when you are if you give me half a chance." She jumped out of bed and shooed them out ahead of her, took a quick shower and joined them as they hurried down the stairs. Ellen felt that she deserved the reputation of being the hospital's quickest dressing nurse.

"Our last breakfast in this joint!" someone exulted. "Believe me from now on I shall have what I want for my morning meal!"

"Somehow, I'm not hungry this morning," another said, as she sipped her tomato juice. "I hate these last affairs— last dance, last day of the year, last—"

"Last good-night kiss," teased someone else. "I thought he would never go, last night."

"Last night! I wasn't even out last night. You're wrong, lady. It must have been two others girls."

Light, inconsequential banter—youth's method of camouflaging deep feeling.

Breakfast over, they trooped into Chapel. Ann and Ellen entered together. The last Chapel before Commencement! To most of the girls it signified little, but to some ten or a dozen it meant the end of their training. The day was theirs for recreation, preparation for the evening, amusement or packing up of belongings before leaving for home or a job as the case might be. Tall jars of Madonna lilies banked the little platform, their scent filling the air. Ellen's eyes swept the room to encounter the blue eyes of young Doctor Dent who stood near the east window talking to the two new internes who had entered the hospital a week before. They smiled briefly across the intervening space and

Ellen sat down in the place she had occupied for nearly three years.

Miss Forsyth entered and walked to the platform. She was followed by the Chief of Staff and the House Physician who took seats on either side of her. The rest of the staff found their places and Miss Forsyth came to the edge of the platform, her finger in the Psalter.

"To most of you who are graduating tonight, this will be the last Chapel meeting. I want you to know that each of you has been a source of joy and inspiration to me. These brief meetings together have never failed to uplift and strengthen me for the arduous duties ahead, and I'm sure you have felt the same way. I could wish that as you leave Anthony Ware, you might feel disposed to continue these morning devotions in whatever field of service you find yourselves. You will discover, as I have, that they grow more precious with the years."

She opened the Psalter. Behind, on either side of her, a white clad man arose. The reading began:

" 'I will lift up mine eyes unto the hills,
     from whence cometh my help'."

The slow, precise voice of Miss Forsyth led in the reading. Again it was the one hundred twenty-first psalm. Clear and strong came the voices of the staff in response:

" 'My help cometh from the Lord, which made
     Heaven and earth'."

Ellen felt her hand grasped convulsively. A long shuddering sigh escaped the girl beside her. Ellen pressed Ann's fingers and leaned closer.

" '—He that keepeth thee will not slumber'."

How beautifully familiar it all was! The erect, handsome Superintendent in fresh, spotless white, her eyes shining as from some inner light; flanked on either side by those two splendid men, so human now and so wonderfully kind! The rows of uniformed nurses, internes, orderlies, dietitian, cook and maids—a goodly company!

Small wonder that eyes glistened as the reading went on to the twenty-third psalm:

" 'The Lord is my Shepherd; I shall not want—' "

Ellen bowed her head. A flood of memories came rushing back. She felt Ann's shoulder against hers and pressed closer in sympathy. Poor Ann! Dear Ann!

Across the intervening heads she could see the smooth blond one of Doctor Cyrus Dent. Beyond him was the great east window—Christ healing the sick—"Freely ye have received—freely give!" The radiance of the morning sun was reflected there. The figures seemed alive—vibrant!

As if he felt her gaze Cy turned, his glance a caress. Happiness enfolded her—the future spread out, full and glorious. Together she and Cy would go on to a life of service. What matter poverty, sacrifice, hardship? The work for which they had spent long, hard years in preparation, was just ahead. They were doing that which they both loved; healing the sick, comforting the broken in spirit, heartening the dying! Just a small town general practitioner and his wife. She felt that she had indeed reached her goal— a trained nurse, fitting helpmeet for her husband—Cyrus Dent, Country Doctor.

THE END

www.ingramcontent.com/pod-product-compliance
Lightning Source LLC
Chambersburg PA
CBHW020134180626
46810CB00004B/1547